The author gratefully acknowledges permission to reprint lyrics from:
"The Model" (Martin/Murdoch/Colburn/Cooke/Geddes/
Jackson/Campbell)
© 2000 Sony/ATV Music Publishing UK Ltd.
All rights administered by Sony/ATV Music Publishing LLC,
8 Music Square West, Nashville, TN 37203.
All Rights Reserved. Used by Permission.

Book design: Eric Rohr • Set in Bell MT

Support independent writers.

www.ginghamblindfold.com

For Lara

And if you think you see with just your eyes you're mad
'Cause Lisa learned a lot from putting on a blindfold
When she knew she had been bad
She met another blind kid at a fancy dress
It was the best sex she ever had

The Model, Belle and Sebastian

Gingham Blindfold

1

There was a wire report about the masturbation rate of eighteen- to twenty-four-year-olds in the United States that ran as a front-page story in the student newspaper where I worked in college. It stated that, every twenty seconds, someone in my age group masturbated.

We received several letters to the editor after the story ran. Some chastised us for putting it on the front page. Others were more jocular, poking fun at the report, saying the number sounded low. A Women's Studies major (all letter writers were required to disclose their major for publication) pointed out the discrepancy between males and females in the survey—males obviously masturbating more than females, as stated in the report. She directed readers to a certain feminist author who encouraged young women to embrace their essence and buy a dildo.

My girlfriend, Kristen, was the only journalism student to argue against running the masturbation story. She didn't think it was informative or funny or a

First Amendment thing. She said it was disgusting. It was inappropriate. At the time, I thought it was possible Kristen had never masturbated.

I still wonder that.

As the paper's editor, I wrote a column in the wake of the report's publication. I mused about how someone might do the deed with privacy, since everyone my age had a roommate, whether they lived in a dorm or an apartment or their parents' basement.

And forget seedy adult bookstores, I wrote. The booths in those things? It was doubtful anyone my age would go near one. Too embarrassing, too degrading. Never mind cleanliness.

There was also a question about the source material. I declared that adult magazines had outgrown their usefulness, given the availability of free porn on the Internet. I backed my thesis with the declining circulation numbers of the more mainstream publications, which I had found in *Editor & Publisher*.

At the end of the column, I concluded that the report's data couldn't possibly be accurate. After all, wasn't this the age when we started getting laid? I pledged to conduct a survey of my own, cheerfully inviting readers to write in with their own experiences.

I had that column on my mind as Kristen was kicking me out. I thought about how much trouble it had caused me when I wrote it, how much trouble it caused me even now, ever since I'd found Indira.

Kristen stormed into the bedroom, where I had been sleeping, and flipped on the lights. "What is this?" she shouted. She was full of rage. "How could you do this to me?"

"Do what?" I asked groggily.

Kristen held up the picture of Indira, the top of which was crumpled in her hand. I heard the washing machine running in the background, and knew she had found it while doing the laundry. She always checked my pockets first.

"It's no big deal," I said calmly, hoping to prevent an escalation. I pulled the sheets over my lap. "It's nothing."

"Then why was it in your pocket? Where did you even get this?" She examined the advertisement on the other side of the page. "This is disgusting."

"It's nothing. It's just a picture, Kristen."

"Just a picture?" Her grip on Indira tightened. All I could do was watch nervously. I certainly couldn't ask for it back. "Yes, clearly this is *just* a picture."

"You're overreacting."

"Am I? It's bad enough that you look at this stuff online, Ethan. And I know you do."

Backed into a corner, I used the same defense I shoe-horned into every argument I had with Kristen since we had moved to California.

"I followed you out here," I argued, the volume of my voice rising. "So cut me some slack."

"I've *been* cutting you slack. And where has it gotten me? This is where." She looked at the ad again. She flipped over the page. And then she was quiet.

"Kristen?"

"You need to get out," she said.

"What do you mean?"

"I mean," she began, a tremble in her voice, "this is over. I want you to move out. I'm sick of this. So sick of it."

"Where am I supposed to go?" I asked breathlessly.

"I don't care."

I threw off the covers and grabbed my jeans off the floor.

"Fine," I snapped, "just cut me a check for my half of the security deposit and I'll be on my way." It was meant to antagonize her, and it did. I had no right to demand it. She'd been spotting me money, it seemed, every day since we'd moved out to California. I owed her more than a security deposit.

"Here's your deposit." She tore the page into pieces and dropped them to the floor. Then she wiped her hands, burst into tears and ran out of the bedroom. There was a hasty gathering of purse and keys, followed by a slam of the front door.

I studied the pieces of paper on the floor, the pieces of tacky typeface, breasts and mouths and erections from the advertisement. The rest of the pieces revealed the damage Indira had sustained. Her right leg was torn and her stomach was ripped at a forty-five degree angle through the middle. Her head was severed from her body. On my way to lock the front door, I stepped over the torn paper like it was a chalk outline at a crime scene.

Running the masturbation story may have angered the newspaper's publishing board—a few old-timers, industry professionals and faculty members—but my column really got them worked up. Even though the university was in Laramie, the liberal bastion of Wyoming, public discussion of masturbation and vibrators and ejaculation still caused a stir.

In fact, there was a movement among the board to

fire me. I thought that was great. Here was a chance to show my mettle as a journalist, someone unwilling to sacrifice principles for a paycheck.

I thought I was pretty hot stuff.

After all, I had been an intern the previous summer at *Record Shelves*, the largest music magazine in the country. I didn't need or, for that matter, want, to be editor of the student newspaper.

But the editor of *The Laramie Daily Democrat*, one of the last family-owned papers in the country, felt differently. The editor was my dad. He hoped I might follow in his footsteps some day, just like he had done with his father before him. He thought that the *Record Shelves* internship would rid me of any wanderlust. When he found that it hadn't, Dad made sure I became student editor. He was nearing retirement age and needed me to be ready to take the reins when they were handed to me. I needed to be ready, whether I wanted them or not.

When the board emerged from the decisive meeting, Dad patted me on the shoulder, smiled smugly and told me that my job was safe. *The Daily Democrat* printed the student newspaper at a substantial discount, and I'm told contract renewal was discussed.

Had Kristen not insisted I take out the trash that evening, I never would have found Indira.

"Ethan," Kristen called from the kitchen for the second time, "come on." She was in a hurry to finish the dishes before the start of "Desperate Housewives."

"In a minute," I replied, my eyes fixed on the computer screen at our shared desk in the dining room. I was surfing the same sites I hit every day at the newspaper, a small daily in Southern California. We had moved there when Kristen accepted a junior position at a public relations firm in San Diego a week after graduation. I packed only what would fit in an oversized equipment bag a friend gave me when he stopped playing hockey. I turned in the keys to the tiny basement apartment I'd had since freshman year, hauled my second-hand furniture to the dump and sold the worn-down Subaru wagon that was once my dad's.

The day before I left, Dad walked me through the newspaper one last time, maybe for sentimental reasons, more likely for guilt. He was trying to show me it was something I would miss, that I couldn't write about rock stars forever. After the farewell tour, he took me to lunch at a greasy spoon around the corner where the newspaper's staff had been eating for years. We ate in silence.

But Dad needn't have worried about my aspirations. After two months without a single freelance record review or rock star profile, I was broke. I reluctantly accepted a position as a copy editor at a small daily. Copyediting was entry-level work. At *The Daily Democrat*, we had high school interns to do the job. But Kristen was no longer willing to cover my half of the rent, and I had to do something.

"Ethan, come on."

"I did it last time," I snapped, not meaning to protest so much as to merely set the record straight. We'd been sniping at each other more often, probably because we hardly saw each other anymore. I worked nights. Kristen worked days. She was always asleep when I came home, leaving me with nothing else to do but drink beer and stare at online porno all night like a statistic in one of my columns. Kristen and I shared a single day off together. And on this particular day, Kristen wanted to stay in. After all, it was a work night for her.

I backed the rolling chair out from the computer desk and laced my sneakers. She stood at the door, waiting for me to unload the rubber trashcan in her hands.

"That's a good boy," she said as I took it.

"Funny," I replied. "But I wouldn't have to take out the trash if we just would have gone out."

"Yes, because it would have just emptied itself while we were having Thai."

"Maybe," I said, sauntering to the door. "Coconut milk has mystical powers."

"It makes you gassy."

"Again, funny." It was our habit to diffuse an argument with gentle sarcasm, and though I was still angry with her, easing the tension was certainly better than being stuck at home and in a fight.

I carried the trash down the cement-block stairs and around the corner of our unit. We lived in a high-density complex called Rancho Margarita. They weren't the greatest apartments, but we signed the lease on the recommendation of the newspaper's columnist, Jasper Markum. Jasper was something of a fixture at Rancho Margarita, a divorcé who was always practicing Spanish with the groundskeepers or watering the potted succulents that lined the sidewalk to his door. As it turned out, Jasper received a discount on his rent for every new tenant he helped to sign. I never told Kristen that he bragged about it one day at work because I figured it would only make matters worse. As it was, she hated that our apartment was so far from the beach, that rap music could be heard at any hour of the day, that our neighbors could probably hear us talking, because we could certainly hear them. But it fit my budget, and we could still smell the floral, salty air wafting from the ocean. Everywhere we looked, there were palm trees. It wasn't so terrible.

I moved down the winding sidewalk that cut through the complex, keeping an eye out for a garbage bin that was a little less full than the rest. I stepped out onto the main street of the complex and in front of an oncoming car, a modified Honda with large chrome rims, primer-gray hood and deafening bass line blasting from its subwoofers. The windows were darkened, and there was something written in an indecipherable Old English script along the top of windshield. The car stopped just in front of me. I stepped backward onto the curb and stood still, clutching the trashcan in my hands. Then, the car slowly moved past me, the dual exhaust meeting the pavement as it rose over a speed bump before suddenly speeding away, a noxious cloud of exhaust and burnt rubber left in its wake.

I continued across the street to the nearest stucco garbage enclosure. I set the can down to tie off the plastic liner, and a to-go box Kristen had forced on top spilled to the ground. I hoisted the bag over the mound of garbage and then knelt down to clean up the mess. As I gathered the wilted lettuce, the tomato slices and the pickles, I saw a magazine under the bin. I wiped my hands on my jeans and reached for it. It was an adult magazine. A porno called *Tight Horizons.*

Finding something like *Tight Horizons,* randomly, and without having to wander shamefully into an adult bookstore or ask the pimply clerk at the gas station made me like I was fifteen and pilfering the Victoria's Secret catalog from the mailbox before Dad got home. I shut the enclosure doors behind me and crouched in the dark behind the enclosure wall. The smell of cantaloupe rinds and soiled diapers ripened the air. I flipped through the pages anxiously. It was difficult to see in the darkness behind the bin, but I could still distinguish the shadowy shapes in the pictures. They were elbows and thighs and breasts. I examined the pages systematically and thoroughly, as though I were trying to memorize each picture to later illuminate in my mind.

I turned the page.

And another.

And then another. And there she was.

I noticed her body first. I can't pretend otherwise. Her breasts were fleshy and round, the edges of her pink nipples blended into her baby-smooth skin. She wore gingham panties. They were red, the kind with white lace around the waist. She was reclined on thick, emerald grass. The feathery ends of her blond hair, reddened by the looming sunset behind her, hung over her shoulders. Her mouth was slightly opened and nearly formed into a smile. She didn't look directly at the camera, but off to the side, to the horizon. Carefully, and repeatedly, I studied her eyes, the arches of her cheekbones and the crinkles on her forehead, the thin creases extending from her eyelids, the color of her skin. I learned her name from the blurb that interrupted the tranquil scene: "Drive your tractor through Indira's barn doors!"

I turned the page for more, but only found an advertisement for "The Rocket," a name that adequately spelled out his talents.

I flipped back to Indira. Immediately, my mind wandered back to the editor's chair at the student paper, pondering in a column the motivations and intentions of anybody who did anything. Indira was such a strange stage name—and surely it was that, because otherwise it would be Michelle or Carla or Samantha. I wondered what drove a woman as beautiful as Indira to put herself in such a position. I figured drugs or poverty or an abusive upbringing, but when I looked into Indira's printed eyes, I saw something else. She seemed at peace with what she did, maybe even happy about it, never mind that it was beneath her.

I didn't know if it was the possibility of rescuing her or touching those breasts, but I wanted to find Indira and tell her she could do better. I was going to help Indira. I was going to help myself.

2

"Ethan, are you out here?" Kristen shouted, her flip flops smacking the pavement as she stormed the grounds of the complex.

I peeked through the crevice of the garbage enclosure doors and saw her carving a path down the middle of the street. Watching Kristen, I was reminded of what I liked best about her. I marveled at the definition of her muscular thighs and the shape of her calves, which were like hot air balloons, her tiny ankles the wicker baskets suspended underneath. Her hair was tied up in a bun, the same way she did it before a shower. She wore my old polka dot boxers and a shrunken pink t-shirt. In college, Kristen preferred tight-fitting jeans or chinos; now that she was a PR flack, she opted for expensive silk suits and bejeweled chains. But at the end of the day, she always wore a skimpy t-shirt and those boxers. She called it her "loungewear."

"Actually, Kristen, it's my loungewear," I would tell her, "you're just living in it."

The boxers were once my favorite pair. It seemed like years had passed since she'd commandeered them, but it was only the end of junior year. We'd been flirting at the student paper the way two journalism majors would flirt, mocking each other's ledes, opening each other's story files and deleting the bylines, changing "its" to "it's" and "theirs" to "there's." One night after the paper had been shipped, the staff darted to a bar across the street to relieve some deadline stress. Hours later, everyone was hammered, most of all our flamboyant entertainment editor. He was dancing on the table, his shirt lifted to show off his round belly, which he smacked to the beat of "Dancing Queen." Kristen and I both feigned disgust and both rose from the table at the same time, presumably to use the toilet. Within seconds, we were in a dark corner of the bar, kissing.

The next morning, I woke to find Kristen digging through the underwear drawer of the dresser next to my bed. I might have protested had I not been so distracted by the way her bikini panties fit snuggly around her cheeks. Kristen took care of herself, at least more than any other girl I had ever been with. She ran compulsively, at least three miles a day, and as a result, her legs were lean and toned. Her skin was light brown from weekly visits to the tanning bed. She used nice lotions that smelled like peaches and honey.

I reached for her rear, but she turned around before I made contact.

"Here," she said, holding my boxers in the air, stretching the waistband taut with both hands. "These will do nicely."

I rarely wore those boxers, saving them for dates or public occasions such as locker rooms or the doctor's office. Had I known a Tuesday night at the paper would end in a make-out session with Kristen, I might have worn them instead of the pinstriped pair with a hole in the crotch that were bunched on the floor along with the rest of the previous night's clothing.

"Why do you need boxers," I asked, sneaking a finger under her panty line, "when you already have briefs?" This time, I successfully snapped the elastic against her thigh. She playfully slapped my hand.

"I hate getting dressed first thing in the morning. I'd rather hang out in my jammies."

"Jammies, huh? What are you, eight?"

She slipped the boxers over her underwear and threw on one of my t-shirts.

"What would you prefer I call them?" she asked, slinking back into bed. She nestled into my arms. "How about loungewear? That wouldn't offend your sleepwear sensibilities, would it?"

"I think loungewear is lovely," I said. "Now take it off."

Kristen neared the garbage enclosure, her keychain pepper spray dangling from her fingers. She probably worried that the way she was dressed would attract unwanted attention.

I folded the picture of Indira—The Rocket ad faced outward—and quietly slipped it into my back pocket. When I was a kid, I used to flatten the colorful boxes my toys came in and hang them over my bed. In high school, I tore out pictures of rock stars from old editions of *Record Shelves* and affixed them to the inside of my locker. I recalled each cherished picture that I had stuck to a wall or a door with just a little

Scotch tape or thumbtacks or Blu Tak. Maybe I would mount Indira on an old piece of cardboard, tape her up some place hidden, where only I could see.

I rolled the magazine tightly and shoved it through a space in the garbage heap. It fell to the bottom of the bin with a dull thud, and I waited to see if the noise alerted Kristen. But she kept walking, either oblivious to the strange sounds coming from behind closed doors or just voluntarily ignorant. I stepped out of the enclosure and crept behind her.

"Hey, baby," I whispered in a dark, disturbing voice I used to annoy her when she was on deadline at the student paper, "you easy?"

Startled, Kristen spun around with the pepper spray pointed at my face. I ducked just before she unleashed a stream of pepper spray, which sent me stumbling backwards onto the ground. When Kristen realized I wasn't a mugger, she burst into laughter. I picked myself up off the ground, rubbed my eyes and checked my skin.

"I'm so sorry!" Kristen tried to stifle her laughter. She pouted her lip and held out the pepper spray like a battered wife who was turning over a gun to the police after shooting her abusive husband. I put my arm around her and gave her a squeeze.

"No, it's a good thing you had it. You shouldn't be out here by yourself at night," I said, covertly checking my pocket. "There's nothing but a bunch of freaks."

I carried the torn pieces to the kitchen table and carefully pieced together Indira, mending the sections with clear tape, making sure to match each and every paper fiber. The pattern of her gingham panties gave me fits, but after several minutes of meticulous repair, Indira was whole again.

I carried her into the bathroom and loosened my pants, my ears on alert for the sound of Kristen returning to the apartment.

When I finished, I cleaned up with a couple of facial tissues that I then flushed down the toilet. I nudged the page away from the sink to a corner of the counter with my elbow so it wouldn't get wet. I washed my hands and dried them thoroughly before I picked up the page. The light magazine stock was sturdier now that I had patched together the pieces of the page, tape strips spread over it like arteries and veins. I folded the page in half and then in fourths, making new creases over the patchwork tape, and stuck it in my pocket, where it felt like a wallet thick with crisp new bills. It was worth as much to me.

I looked for fresh clothes, but everything I usually wore was soaking wet in the washing machine. I reached into Kristen's closet and dug through a box of old clothes meant for charity. I put on threadbare boxers, a pair of jeans and my old *Record Shelves* t-shirt, the only compensation I had received as an intern. I began to pack. I grabbed my wet clothes out of the washer and stuffed them inside my old hockey bag. Some of Kristen's socks and underwear fell to the ground, but I left them. I walked back inside the apartment and shoved shelves of CDs on top of the wet clothes, followed by pictures of Kristen and me that I ripped from the refrigerator door. I tore down ticket stubs of concerts and movies we'd seen from a corkboard on a wall in the bedroom, tacks flying onto the mattress like shrapnel. I searched under the bed for any refugees: a sock, a favorite pen, a Wet-Nap from the Thai restaurant. Spare change in between the couch cushions went into my pockets. Sticky notes went into the bag. Food went into my stomach. This wasn't about me forgetting somebody. This was about me being forgotten. I was erasing my existence, stealing from Kristen any opportunity for our memories to linger in her brain. It felt violent. It felt like war.

I reached under the bed for my tattered shoebox of clips, where I kept copies of the masturbation column. I sealed the box with packing tape and forced it on top of the pile in the bag. I zipped it shut, flung it over my shoulder and carried it outside.

After I locked the deadbolt, I stuck the key in an envelope stolen from the stash Kristen used to pay bills and write letters, and shoved it under the door. It skidded across the vinyl floor and bumped against the edge of the carpet runner.

I heaved the bag over my shoulder, and a corner of the clip box dug into my skin. But I carried it just the same. I had a long way to go, and the pain wasn't unbearable. I had felt worse.

3

There was another girl like Indira, but I hadn't found her in an adult magazine.

Her name was Tabitha. We shared a class together during freshman year, "Intro to German." There wasn't anything breathtaking or exotic about Tabitha—in fact she may have been the opposite. Her ears weren't pierced. She had a pug nose and jowly cheeks. Her hair was brown and cut medium length. She wore patterned summer blouses and chino skirts that crowned her stubby legs. The most noticeable thing about her was her bright orange backpack, which was covered with patches of European flags, slogans in foreign languages and a label from a Nutella jar.

I wondered what the slogans meant and where she had gotten the patches. Maybe she'd railed across Europe—something I'd always wanted to do—but it was hard to imagine this girl waiting for a train in Berlin with that backpack slung over her shoulder, standing out like a stray traffic cone on the Autobahn.

And yet her language skills were excellent. When the teacher's assistant called on Tabitha, she always earned his highest praise: "*Sehr gut!*"

A few weeks into the semester, I arrived late to class and found that everyone had broken into groups. Tardiness had become a habit of mine, the result of late nights spent press-checking *The Daily Democrat*. The T.A. warned that another tardy would result in my final grade dropping a full letter. Satisfied that I understood the severity of the situation, he told me to join any group with an odd number. I hurried over to the far corner of the classroom, where Tabitha was busily coaxing answers to the workbook's banal questions about color preferences and telephone manners from others in the group. A few of them mumbled half-hearted attempts before turning their attention to the clock. The rest were discussing a recent fraternity party that the cops had busted the weekend before.

I grabbed a chair from an empty desk next to Tabitha, and the hardened rubber ends of the legs squeaked as I dragged it across the linoleum floor. I hurriedly dug through my bag, searching for my workbook. The kind of day I was having, of course I'd forgotten it.

"That's OK," Tabitha said, handing me hers.

"*Vielen dank*," I replied. She seemed rather pleased that I had answered in German, as if it was a second language to me. But it was just a formal variation of "thank you" I had taken to saying because everybody knew "*danke schoen*," and I thought it made me unique.

I scanned the open workbook, and Tabitha pointed to the middle of the page where the group had left off. I read and reread the question to myself before I made a public attempt.

"*Wie ist mein Akzent?*" I asked.

"*Nicht so gut, es tut mir leid, zu sagen,*" she replied.

I had no idea what she had said, but it sounded great. I asked her if she already spoke German, and when she nodded, I asked her why she didn't just pay for the credits and test out of the class.

"If I'm paying for the credits, shouldn't I get something out of it? Now, *Bitte, wo ist die toilette?*" Then, with a giggle, she whispered, "I don't want to pee my pants."

We took turns asking questions, and while she scribbled answers in her workbook, I watched the way she dotted her *I*s and *J*s with bubbles like she was a fifth-grader, that mousy brown hair swishing in front of her face. I listened intently to her answers and the way that she spoke. I imagined the two of us wandering through the German countryside, Tabitha strapped into her orange backpack, using her language skills to befriend the locals, confer with cab drivers and order our meals.

By mid-terms, I had worked up the nerve to ask her out. I lingered after class while Tabitha tucked the day's worksheet neatly into her book.

"I'm Ethan Ames." I held out my hand.

"I know, silly." She had learned my name from group, of course, but I had no idea how to initiate a social conversation other than to robotically pretend this was our first encounter. "But it's nice to meet you again, Ethan."

"Where are you from?" I asked.

"Florida."

"That right? It's warm there." I might as well have been speaking German.

"Yes." She paused. "I guess it is."

"Why did you come to Wyoming?"

"I just wanted a change. I like spending time in different places," she said sweetly. "I like to explore."

"Right. I saw the patches." I pointed to the bag. "You've been to Europe? I'd like to go some time."

"You have to. I was an exchange student in high school. It's lovely."

"Maybe you could tell me about it some time. Maybe over coffee?"

"*Klinkt prachtig.*" Tabitha said as she put her book in her backpack.

"Is that German?"

"Time for you to hit the books, Ethan," she teased. "That was Dutch."

"Wow, how many languages do you know? I'll need a tutor just to keep up," I hinted.

"*Klinkt prachtig,*" she repeated.

"Yes?"

She hoisted her backpack over her shoulders.

"*Klinkt prachtig*—sounds wonderful."

The first night Tabby tutored me, we only studied for an hour before we got bored and decided to make doughnuts and watch "The Simpsons." From there we split our time evenly between homework and ditching class to play tag football or eat waffles at a crummy truck stop diner. She bought me a pot of herbs and a heat lamp because she thought I was a good cook. She tickled me on the nose and called me "The Music Man." She knocked on my door early on the weekend to go running because she wanted me to kick my smoking habit.

I was pretty hooked.

Most nights, after we'd finished the requisite study hour, we ordered a pizza and discussed weekend plans. I suggested the football game or a day trip to Denver. Suddenly, Tabitha became very excited, and strangely, a little nervous. She asked if I wanted to attend a gathering of Christian students on campus. They had started meeting on Saturdays, she said, and she would like to go. This was the first time I'd heard Tabitha mention anything about religion, and I thought she was being sarcastic. I thought she meant it as a joke.

"That could be fun," I said. "Those Suzie Sunshine hymns always crack me up. We could sing all bad and off-key or something to screw with them."

Tabitha became sullen, and I quickly apologized. When I saw her bow her head before she grabbed a slice, just like she had when we went out for waffles, I started to get the idea.

That Saturday, we met at the small auditorium in the student union. It was packed. Tabby sought out a group standing in the back of the room and introduced me to a guy named Shag. He told me repeatedly how "awesome" it was that I came, and did I know how "awesome the Lord's love is?" The tinny strumming of a twelve-string guitar projected through large speakers on either side of the stage. Everyone stopped talking. A buzz of a bass line came through a speaker behind me. A student clad in a low-cut dress and a headset walked on stage and sang "The Lord's Prayer" in a pious soprano, and hundreds of hands reached into the air. I moved toward the doors and hid in the corner of the auditorium, smirking throughout the performance. Tabitha saw me: I made sure of it.

I wasn't a stranger to church. Dad and I attended pretty regularly, in fact. In a small town, it was an editor's job to be an upstanding member of the community, and my dad felt a public obligation to do those kinds of things. But we never talked about church at home. We didn't read the Bible. I was sent to Sunday school with almost a wink and a nudge. Church was a pleasant experience, if a mix of mysticism, morality and wishful thinking. Maybe I couldn't handle the Saturday night crowd, but church I could do.

"You don't need to go," Tabitha said over the phone as she was getting ready on a Sunday morning. She had not invited me.

"I will. If it will make you happy," I said, "I'll do it."

"That's okay."

"Well, if you're okay with it."

"It's fine, Ethan."

Not long after that, she left for a week-long Bible study in the Big Horn Mountains. Tabitha didn't call to say goodbye before she left, but she did call when she came back. I was at her door within minutes. I had missed her like crazy. I'd even read a bit of the Gospels while she was away, as if they would bring me closer to her.

"Let's take a walk," she said, grabbing my hand. I should have seen it coming, but I was oblivious. I thought we were just going for a stroll. I wanted to tell her about my recent reading.

There was a park nearby where we had spent so many early mornings stamping out my smoking habit, and we sat at a picnic table under an oak tree where we once ate orange slices after a jog. I thought maybe Tabitha would have fiddled with her fingers or stared silently at the bird crap on the table while she figured out what to say. But as soon as we sat down, she did it. She had no problem finding the words. She had known what to say for a while.

I didn't give up on Tabitha, though. One night, I drunkenly sauntered to her dorm room and thumped on her door. Tabitha listened patiently as I preached about the depth of my feelings for her. I don't remember much of it, but I woke up early that morning, snuggled in her arms, both of us fully clothed on top of the bed. During our time dating, we had never spent the night together, had hardly kissed. She could have kicked me out, but she didn't. The gesture encouraged me, even though the following hours were awkward. I was hung over and she was distant.

Over the next two years, I kept tabs on Tabitha's various boyfriends, chatted her up when I saw her at the student union and registered for religion courses I knew she'd take, hoping she'd be my study partner.

But at the start of senior year, the e-mails I sent to Tabitha's address bounced back, and her phone number was disconnected. I didn't see her at the union. Desperate, I went to her Saturday night church group and found Shag.

"Dude," he said, grabbing my shoulder congenially, "she's on a year-long mission."

Tabitha never came back. The last I heard, she married a minor soccer player in Holland, had twin baby girls and spoke fluent Dutch.

Standing there in the middle of that room, listening to a contemporary Christian rock band search for salvation in the chords of a Pearl Jam song, I thought about waking up in Tabitha's arms. Now I knew her embrace wasn't a tender one. It wasn't really even protective. It was patronizing.

"Hey, dude, are you going to mosh?" Shag asked me.

I looked at him blankly. My throat was clenched.

"It's okay, we can mosh," he said. "The Lord thinks moshing is awesome."

"Awesome."

4

There was a Motel 6 down the street from the apartment that I walked past every night on my way home from work. The number three on the motel's sign that faced the highway was burned out, making it appear as though a single-bed room cost only nine dollars when it was actually thirty-nine. The sign had been that way since I'd come to Oceanside, and the motel's reluctance to fix it would have driven my dad crazy. *The Daily Democrat* had a small illuminated sign on a xeriscaped mound in front of the building, and leaving one night after press check, we saw a dark spot behind the "Daily." Dad would be back at the paper the next morning, but he refused to let it wait till then.

He went back inside the office for a package of light bulbs. Using a screwdriver pulled from the ice-encrusted trunk of our car, he unscrewed the bolts from the glass face and laid it gently on a fresh drift of snow while I complained about being tired and freezing. I was in high school and prone to the usual teenage mood swings and tantrums, so Dad spared me the lecture, or perhaps himself the headache. He simply spoke to himself as though he was a pastor delivering a sermon to an empty sanctuary. Every detail counted, every correctly spelled caption, every reader complaint heeded, every light bulb replaced. I rolled my eyes at the time, aching to get out of the cold and into my warm bed. And yet I couldn't help but hear my dad's voice as I walked across the street into the motel's parking lot. What did that burned-out sign say about the motel? What other corners did they cut? Did they leave dirty sheets on the bed? Did the maids not wipe down the toilets or replace the water glasses?

There was a story that ran in the paper recently about the dirty habits of hotel maids. Captured on hidden camera around the country were maids rinsing used glasses in the bathroom sink, wiping them out with facial tissue and replacing them on the counter as if they were fresh from the dishwasher. They did all of this, of course, while wearing the same yellow rubber gloves they'd used while scrubbing the toilets. Though it had all been caught on tape (we ran a still from some of the footage), every single hotel owner denied that such housekeeping practices occurred on their premises. I think some of the hotel owners were sued, but I don't remember what happened. Maybe they settled. Maybe they just fired the maids.

I walked into the front office. There were no other customers, only a clerk at the front desk. He was focused on something behind the counter, his arms moving side to side like he was on an assembly line.

"I'd like a room."

"Just a minute, son," he said, like I was a teenager

asking the old man for a little money and the keys to the Olds. "New to Oceanside?"

"Mostly."

He nodded, continuing with his activities behind the counter. He wore a faded blue Oxford, unbuttoned at the top, the dog tags chained around his neck buffered by the fluffy, silver hair on his chest. His sleeves were rolled past his elbows, exposing a green tattoo of a hula girl on one forearm and an anchor with some illegible writing on the other. His hair was cut in a buzz, with thick sideburns that extended to his earlobes. He looked like a retired Marine. There were dozens just like him everywhere you turned in Oceanside. They came to Camp Pendleton as young men, did their tours, dutifully obliged every base transfer, and then retired back on the coast. They knew a good thing when they saw it.

"There we go now." He plopped a stack of white, hot pink and sea green letter-sized paper on the counter. "I apologize for the wait. You need a room? One night?"

I looked at the top sheet. "Missing" was written in large black type across the top. Below it was a grainy, photocopied picture of a pretty girl with round apple cheeks and pixie-like short hair. The text underneath said her name was Bethany. She was last seen in Southwest Riverside County. Her date of birth was a few months after mine.

"Is this someone you know?"

"Dean's kid. He works here, Dean. I'm pulling a double so he can look for her. I thought these fliers might help."

"Is it serious?"

"Sure, it's serious." He said it like someone's pet goldfish had died. "Well, for my friend Dean, it's serious. Bethany's always been trouble."

"I hope she's OK."

He shrugged. "I don't think she's gone too far."

"You don't?"

He cleared his throat. He'd said too much. "Well, now, no need to involve a customer in other folks' problems."

"But if you don't think it's that serious," I said, "why did you make all of these?"

"Because Dean is my friend. How long will you be staying with us?"

"I guess indefinitely."

"I'll book you for tomorrow. Let us know if you change your mind. No refunds after four. This cash, credit, debit? We don't take checks."

I paused. "Credit." I handed over my card.

"Now, if you were staying here tomorrow, you might just bump into Dean. I imagine he'll be back by then."

"Alright."

"Alright. So I'd hate for you to tell him what I've told you."

"I won't tell him anything."

"You're saying I can trust you, then?" He hunched over the counter, squinting his eyes like he was scoping for Viet Cong. "I've got your word, then?"

"You have my word." I added a "Sir" as though we were speaking in some military code.

"You know what I think," he read my credit card, "Ethan Ames?"

I shook my head, suddenly wishing I hadn't handed it over to him.

"I think the little bitch went to L.A. to flash her tits

in some skin flick."

Chuck didn't have anyone else to share his theory with. His wife's been gone for twenty years. Died after breast cancer spread into her lungs. And forget the kids. They don't talk to him anymore.

"They live like a bunch of goddamn hippies in the People's Republic of Berkeley."

Sometimes he talked to the guy at the corner gas station, the checkout girl at Ralphs. The paperboy. But Dean was the person he talked to most. Who else could he tell his story to, then?

Me, I guess. And his story was this:

Chuck went by coffee time, the way some people are able to set their internal alarm clocks or discern the time of day by the position of the sun. He actually wore a watch, an old silver timepiece with the flexible metal strap, but he never looked at it except with loving affection. The watch didn't work anymore. But it was a gift from his late wife, and he'd just as soon stop wearing his wedding ring. There was no need for the watch to keep time anyway. He drank the same amount of coffee every day, at the same pace, at the same hours. Coffee time. A watch that worked would only be redundant.

When his third cup of coffee was half empty, the remnants gone cold, he knew it was time to count the register. Chuck tallied the credit card clips first, stacking them into a neat pile and fastening them with a paperclip. The next step was always more difficult. Chuck was dyslexic as a child. Counting a series of nearly identical ones, fives, tens and twenties was a challenge, and one that required his undivided attention. When he began the procedure, carefully matching receipts to the cash in the register, repeating the growing amount in his head after each bill he laid down on the counter, the door jingled. Chuck didn't look up. He didn't need to. He knew it was Dean. Chuck threw his hand in the air, a half-hearted wave that was his habit. "Three hundred twenty-seven," Chuck whispered to himself.

Chuck almost lost count when a small hand slapped against his own in a raucous high five. Dean had never given him a high five before, only shook his hand, and his palms weren't soft, either. He didn't wear jewelry, and he didn't smell like bubblegum and beach sweat.

"Whatcha doin', Chuck?"

It was Bethany, dressed in a skimpy bikini top and cutoff Levi's. Chuck could see the bottom of her butt hanging out of them in the reflection on the glass doors behind her. Bethany leaned over the counter, her tender cleavage begging him to stare. She'd grown up so fast, Chuck thought.

Bethany smacked her gum and told Chuck she needed a room.

"I don't have time for games," he told her. "I'm a little busy, and your daddy's going to be here any second." Chuck repeated "three hundred twenty seven" in his head, trying not to lose track of the drawer money. "Three hundred twenty, three hundred... shit, was it thirty?"

There was loud music coming from a black Dodge Ram parked in front of the office, the motor still running. The windows were rolled down. Two girls cavorted in the back seat of the cab, laughing and kicking the head rests with their bare feet. They were either drunk or high. Chuck sensed trouble.

"What do you need a room for? They with you?"

Bethany backed away from the counter. She chomped her bubble gum and grinned.

"Maybe. What are you gonna do about it?"

What was he going to do about it? What could he do?

"Those girls drinkin'?"

Motel rules gave Chuck the right to refuse a room to anyone who appeared intoxicated. Bethany was sober, though, even if she was making the choices of a drunken idiot.

She waved at the truck. "No sir!" She saluted him.

A good Marine, he couldn't bend the rules. He took her cash, which was scrunched into several wads, and slipped a keycard into the paper holder, scribbling the room number on top. He wrote her name in the log as Betsy B. Good.

"I'm still tryin' to figure out how I came up with such a funny name so damn quick," Chuck told me.

Bethany took the keycard and leapt into the truck. Chuck had lost count of the drawer and was forced to start over. Carelessly but not uncaring, he hurried through his chore, so he could rush out the door when Dean arrived. This was not their habit, and Chuck would need to explain why he'd been so curt with his good friend. But he couldn't think about it right then. When he got home, he guzzled a twelve of Pabst, smoked a pack of Kool Menthols and devoured a heaping turkey-and-pepper-jack sandwich that gave him heartburn the remainder of the night.

The next morning, Chuck set out for work on his Harley. The sun-soaked seat singed his crotch, intensifying his hangover. He shifted restlessly on the searing leather as he roared down the road to the motel. This was nothing, Chuck thought. His ass would hurt twice as bad when Dean kicked it. One less friend, Chuck thought. He never imagined old age would be so lonely.

Chuck parked his bike and removed his helmet. When he went inside the front office, Dean was waiting behind the counter, smiling wearily.

"Hey buddy," Dean said. "You're early. I might just get home for 'Teletubbies.'"

Chuck laughed nervously. "Any problems last night, Dean-O?"

"Nah, pretty quiet."

Relieved, Chuck rubbed the worry out of his face. It reminded him of a game he played with his kids. "Turn that frown," he'd tell them, changing expressions as he moved his hand back and forth, "upside down!"

There was a fresh pot of coffee on the counter. Chuck poured some into a Styrofoam cup.

"Got a couple complaints about noises in 203. I called down there to tell 'em to shut up and some chick answered, all out of breath." Dean licked his lips. "Like to get me some of that."

Chuck didn't say a word. He drank the entire cup at once, burning his throat and throwing off his schedule.

"You don't want a piece of this, Dean-O," Chuck whispered to himself, standing in the doorway of room 203 after the maids had called him down to show him the mess.

Beer cans, empty liquor bottles and Trojan wrappers

littered the carpet. Chuck kicked empty film canisters as he walked into the bathroom. Spent condoms and tissue clogged the toilet. The chrome faucet on the counter outside of the bathroom was coated with greasy smears, and there were lipstick kisses on the mirrors. The place reeked of body odor and bad breath.

Chuck stepped outside for a breather. He had barely lit his cigarette when one of the maids called out in broken English.

"Christ, what is it now?"

She handed him a toiletry bag from under the vanity. Chuck couldn't count the panicked calls he'd received from guests who were halfway to Arizona before realizing they'd left behind a purse, a piece of luggage, a toiletry bag. He looked inside. There was a package of disposable razors, strawberry-flavored lubricant, condoms and a glass dildo. There was also a stack of Polaroids. They were of Bethany, on the very bed Chuck was standing next to, her legs spread, the dildo in her mouth, the dildo rubbing against her face, the dildo inserted.

"Clean it up," he told the maids, shoving the photos back into the bag. "Clean it up now."

Chuck carried the bag to the dumpster, withdrew several trash bags and threw it inside. He replaced the bags and shut the dumpster lid.

"Dean don't think she's a saint," Chuck told me at the end of his story, "believe me. But he don't know how bad she is, either. Thing is, Ethan Ames," he said, again reading my name on my credit card, "I don't have the heart to tell him."

He tapped it on the stack of fliers. "That's why I'm making these for my friend Dean."

I reached out for my card and key, and Chuck snapped to attention.

"Shoot, you don't want to hear about other people's problems. Here you go. Just do me a favor. Keep this between you and me."

"I will." I looked down at the keycard envelope. It was blank. "What room am I in?"

Chuck flashed a grin, sideburn to sideburn. "You're in 203."

I swiped the keycard through the door lock, waited for the blinking green light below the handle and stepped inside. There was the faintest smell of smoke, even though the room was designated non-smoking. I turned on the light, set my bag on a luggage rack in the closet and inspected my new surroundings. Permanent hangers were neatly tucked to one side of the coat rack. The top square of toilet paper on the rung was folded into a triangle. The soaps were nestled in their wrappers and placed at an angle along three arranged plastic-wrapped cups, which I found to be a relief. There weren't chocolates on the pillows, but the room had an order to it and a superficial cleanliness, familiar and generic. It was a motel room, same as any other.

I removed the picture of Indira from the bulging hockey bag and laid it down on the sienna-colored comforter. Almost immediately, I became erect. The grotesque images on the back of the page no longer bothered me. I had chosen to ignore that side of her. I went quickly, eager for release.

5

When I walked into work the next day, my supervisor, Clark, was busy proofing an entertainment page. Clark was an old guy who'd been in the newspaper business a long time. He used to run a small daily in Montana that, he grumbled, was ruined after its purchase by a corporate chain. Unwilling to tolerate the hierarchy of corporate overlords, Clark uprooted his wife and teenage son to seek out warmer winters and better pay in California. Clark was a sharp newspaperman—he should have been more than just a night editor—but already near retirement age, he was too cynical for upward movement. I saw Clark, I saw my dad, and then I saw myself in twenty years, and wondered how anyone could expect me to follow in either of their footsteps.

I greeted Clark, who replied with a simple nod, and threw down my pack. The newsroom was quietly pulsing; all the city editors, beat reporters and clerks had weekend hangovers and were just grinding it out until the end of the day. I slipped into my swivel chair and turned on my Mac. The buzz of the computer coming to life drew the attention of a harried reporter on the other side of my cubicle, but he quickly returned to the story on his screen.

I checked my messages. There were a few mass e-mails from the executive editor in Escondido, one from Clark about leaving before I did a press check leftover from the weekend and some junk mail. Nothing from Kristen. We'd hardly ever gone for more than a day without speaking to each other, even if we'd just had a spat over the phone when she was out of town. I figured this latest bout was just another bit of theater, the kind we always acted out before reconciling with sex or a trip to the bar. Didn't she wonder where I had gone? Apparently not. And for that, I was relieved. It was like we'd crossed a critical threshold that had defied us for so long. I grabbed a red pen and a proof out of the wire basket and got to work. Clark tapped me on the shoulder.

"Want to enter any of these headlines in the CAL Awards?" Clark asked in his ambling drawl, holding a handful of tear sheets. The CAL Awards were the biggest journalism competition in the state.

"Not especially." I wasn't proud of the pages. This was just copyediting, and I was a writer.

"Didn't think so." He reached over to his desk and exchanged the tear sheets with the day's proofs. "Here're your pages, dude."

I set them aside and opened a story by Elizabeth Anderson Carlisle, the paper's best reporter. Liz covered hospital board meetings, physician scandals and the latest anti-depressant trends in Los Angeles.

Then she'd dig up stories on ruthless pimps or pen advocacy pieces about the need to supply junkies with clean needles. Liz had already won the CAL Award twice, for her reporting on strung-out prostitutes in Los Angeles and teenage pornography in San Diego. She was only a couple years older than me.

Judging by the initials in the editing column, the story had been read by several editors. But I was going to read it anyway. Everybody wanted to read Liz's stuff. Some because it was easy—her copy was clean, so it was an easy way to get your initials on a story before a smoke break. Others wanted to read it because they had a hard on for Liz. I think I read her stories out of a competitive urge, but I don't know where the competition was. Liz was in a league above me—a league above all of us, really.

"Are you in my story?" Liz asked, startling me. I was so engrossed, I hadn't noticed her standing at my desk.

The story was about a husband who had cheated on his wife, contracted HIV and then knowingly passed it on to her. He was facing criminal charges, but the kicker of the story was that his wife didn't want him prosecuted. After all, she *was* still sleeping with the guy. Liz quoted an Assemblyman who wanted to disregard the wife's wishes, making a perpetrator like the husband automatically liable for passing on the disease to a spouse.

"I'm sorry," I said.

"Don't be sorry. Can you close it? I need to add a quote."

"Why do you stick around this dump, Liz?" Clark asked, turning around in his chair. He is, by some strange bit of luck, friends with her outside of work. "You should be working in L.A." He said it loud enough for our editor to hear.

It was a valid question. There were rumors that after the CAL Awards, Liz received a sizeable raise. The publisher was apparently worried that she would jump ship. But a paper of our size didn't often wrangle over reporters' salaries—they couldn't afford to. That led others to think it was family money that was bankrolling Liz, because she clearly had it coming from somewhere. She dressed well, she was a little too generous with picking up the tab for takeout or drinks, and she drove a Porsche 356 Speedster, black, always waxed and shining, right down to the bullet rims. It was easily the nicest car in the parking lot, and not one that many could afford in the business. The second nicest car in the lot was Jasper's Camaro, and it was a piece of shit. Clark said her Speedster was a collector's car, and he grumbled about her driving it every day. "It belongs in a garage," he said, though never to her face. None of us were quite ballsy enough to ask her where or how she had acquired such a vehicle.

"L.A., Clark?" Liz asked him, leaning against the cubicle wall along my desk. "This is as close to L.A. as I want to be. Close *enough.*"

I closed the file on my computer screen. "I'm out. Let me know when you're done."

"Thanks," she said with a wink. "It'll just take a sec'." Liz returned to her desk, and I watched everyone watch her. She was wearing a chino skirt, a lacy green tunic and black mules. She looked good.

Her auburn hair was long and full-bodied. The copy desk joked with her that she should quit writing and become a shampoo model. ("Or a nude model," Clark always chimed in, with total disregard for sexual harassment laws.) Liz has probably never had a zit. Her eyes are big and brown, her shoulders slight but assured. Liz smelled nice and always wore silver jewelry. She was so confident that she could deflate anyone's ego with her command of a room. And she endeared herself to the desk, a hard task. Copy editors generally viewed the rest of the newsroom with equal parts jealousy and contempt. When it was late at night and the desk was behind schedule, Liz would stick around to help us get the paper out, even though the other reporters had gone home.

"Ethan," she called out, and I was surprised that she knew my name, although I shouldn't have been. It was a small newsroom and I'd been there long enough. "Ready."

When I went to edit the story again, it was locked, and I knew our editor had opened the file. He wasn't the only one who tried. I heard someone whisper "fuck." Elsewhere I heard a huff.

I looked over to Liz, who was now on the phone, oblivious to the quiet rivalry for editing rights to her story. I continually refreshed my computer while I absentmindedly proofed the community news page. Eventually, I got lucky. A little lock graphic next to the story slug changed to an unlocked image, but when I double-clicked it, the screen refreshed and it was locked again. "Fuck," I said now. The managing editor looked over and smiled smugly. Maybe he was just screwing with us.

When I finally got back into her story, there were two new sets of initials added to the list. This was getting ridiculous. I figured I should probably close it, but I wanted to finish the rest of the story, even if there was nothing left to edit. When I got to the final quote, though, I sensed trouble. I scribbled the quote on a sticky note, hit "save" and left the file open. I waited for Liz to hang up before I walked over to her desk.

"Hey, Liz."

"What's up?" she asked, looking up from a sentence she was reading through bookish, thick-rimmed glasses.

"I just finished that story. It's really good."

"Thanks," she said, warmly.

"But I'm worried about this quote."

"Which one?"

I read from the sticky note, "'There are some things you can legislate, but it ain't love or a lay.' That's pretty good."

"Isn't that *terrible*? That's the one I just added," Liz said. "I couldn't believe this lady said that. I mean, *hello*, your cheating husband just gave you HIV. You know that's, like, a bad thing, right? Doesn't it just feel like a Tammy Wynette song on steroids? Is she standing by her man or what?"

"Yeah, it's crazy. But I'm not sure it will make it past the final edit, this being a family paper and all."

"You don't think so?" she asked, and I shook my head to confirm. "No, I suppose you're right." Liz slumped in her seat. She wasn't pouting, but it was obvious she took this stuff seriously.

"What do you propose we do?" she asked. "It's a good quote. I want it in there."

I checked my watch and looked at the clock.

"Well, if you put it in the middle, it might get missed

by those guys," I said, pointing at the editor, who was conferring with his second-in-command. "They read a lot of copy all day. I'm sure when it's this close to deadline they just skim."

I knew this because my dad told me to be careful in the late afternoon when it's deadline time, copy is pouring in and I was tired.

"Besides," I continued, "your stuff's always so clean." The hairs on the back of my neck tingled. My ears reddened.

Liz sat up and smiled. "That's so sweet."

"I just meant that—"

"Good idea, Ethan," she said, touching the side of my arm. "Let's try it."

At work the next day, Liz caught me in the lobby on my way to the restroom.

"The quote survived!"

"Yeah, I saw. Pretty cool."

"Much beer do I owe you, though I, of course, prefer a martini. Dry and dirty. Let's go tonight."

My heart went into a freefall from the thirtieth floor. Indira who?

"I can stand to be in no man's debt. You get off at ten-thirty? I'll be up," she said, putting on a light sweater on her way out the door. "I never sleep."

I could imagine. "OK."

"We'll meet at Palace Bar. It's next door in Carlsbad. Do you know the place?"

"I do. But, actually, could you pick me up?" I reddened. "I don't have a car."

"Wow. No, good for you," she said. "Sure. You know what? Maybe I'll just stick around then and help out the desk."

"Oh, you don't have to do that. I could walk, or maybe even catch the bus or something."

"No way. I'll wait for you. I want to."

6

"I did it again, didn't I?" Liz said as she polished off her second martini. "I just interrupted. I do that when I drink. Devil liquor!"

"That's OK." I was nervous and had been speaking short sentences most of the night. Liz noticed.

"Get this man another beer," she shouted to the bartender. "He's drying up."

The bartender plopped a pint on my wet bar napkin. "Another one, Lizzy?" She nodded.

"He's the only one I let call me Lizzy," she confided. "I don't really like it. My name is Liz. When you read the paper, it's Elizabeth. Simple. But it *is* Greg..."

There was a twinkle in her eye. I wondered if she was sleeping with the guy. I could see it.

"Not so fast, mister. It ain't like that." She hit me on the arm mischievously.

"He's *gay*," she whispered. "Now, tell me more about yourself, Mr. Ames. I demand it. And try to put a few more syllables in there this time."

"Huh?"

She hit me on the arm again. "Funny. So? You wrote for *Record Shelves*, right? What was that like?"

"It was good. It was really good."

"How did you end up out here then?"

"Well—"

"Oh, right." Liz fictitiously cleared her throat. "Kristen."

I tilted my head. "How do you know about Kristen?"

She chewed on an olive and grinned.

"I see. Well, yeah, anyway, so here I am. It's been a strange time. I came out here expecting to write, but it's not happening. I at least thought I'd have a beat by now."

"There are plenty of opportunities to write at this paper. You just have to be patient."

"But I shouldn't have to wait," I argued. "They told me I needed to work the desk for a year before they'd give me a beat, but Jessica Munford got one after four months."

"I agree, it's a little unfair." She twisted the stem of her freshened martini glass.

"Oh, God," I replied. "I hear a 'but' coming."

"Well, *yeah*, of course there is a 'but.' I think you're just going to have to play the game until you can show the editors what you're capable of."

"I thought a lifetime of summer internships under my dad was a good example of what I'm capable of. I thought writing for *Record Shelves* was a pretty good example of what I'm capable of."

Liz sipped the top of her martini like it was hot coffee. "I think newspaper editors are going to be a little snobby about a music magazine like *Record Shelves*. Sorry."

"I guess. Sometimes I wonder why I came out here."

"You sure have had a rough go of it lately," she said with a laugh to lighten the moment. "Speaking of which, where are you staying now that you're home-less?"

"The Motel 6," I said.

"Cozy."

She took another sip from her martini and spilled a little on her shirt. She hastily dabbed at the spill with a bar napkin. I pretended not to notice. I looked up at the grungy ceiling of the Palace Bar. The paint was peel-ing along the crown molding. I let slip a yawn. It had been a long haul at the paper—we had to tear apart the front page at the last minute for a breaking story on a house fire in De Luz—and I was wiped.

Liz grabbed her bag from the bar rail and dug around for her keys.

"How drunk are you?" she asked.

"Not very."

"Why don't you drive me home? I probably shouldn't get behind the wheel. You can just crash there. Beats a Motel 6. Have you ever driven a 356?"

She put a couple twenties on the bar and waved to Greg. "Let's go."

"Liz, I can't let you pay—"

"Let's go," she said with a wink, intentionally inter-rupting me.

"Alright." I took the keys from her bejeweled hand. "Let's go."

"Pretty great, isn't it?" Liz shouted, her hair tugged by the wind. I watched for cops as I cruised the Speedster over El Camino Real.

"It's pretty rad," I yelled, embarrassed to suddenly be speaking like a skateboarder.

"I like that." She slammed her hand on top of the passenger door. "It is pretty rad!"

"If you don't mind me asking, how did you get such a cool car? Are you loaded?" That was the beer talking.

She feigned shock that I would ask her such a question.

"My dad used to race these. He raced them in the Fifties and Sixties. He was pretty famous, I guess. He met his first wife at a race at Torrey Pines."

"Your mom?" I asked.

"No," she said shyly. "My mom was his second wife. Get this, he actually cheated on his first wife with my mom."

"You know what that makes you?" I waited for a reaction.

"Indescribably original?"

"A love child!" I thought it would sound clever and ironic, but as soon as I said it, I wondered if I had no business being behind the wheel. "You don't meet one of those everyday."

"No, you sure don't," she chuckled. "Wait, you're not one, are you?"

I shook my head. "Nope."

She smirked. "Anyway, he wanted kids, but they never had any. She couldn't. So he parked all of his cars in a big barn near Lake Elsinore and focused on the family steel business. It's no wonder he cheated. I think he needed to feel alive. But he took care of his first wife. There were no pre-nups back then, you know. She died a couple years ago, actually. Quite wealthy."

Liz gazed upward at the night sky. She rolled her

head wearily,

"But my dad showed me and my mom a life we'd otherwise never have known." It seemed like she wasn't talking to me really, but was merely broadcasting an inner dialog with herself. "When he died, he left me this. They say I shouldn't drive it, but I don't listen to them. Dad told me it would be mine some day, but he made me promise I'd never lock it up in some old barn like he did."

"You must have some gin tucked away in a second stomach somewhere," I chided her. "I think you're drunker than when we left."

When I downshifted, she grabbed my hand and squeezed.

"I had a lot of fun tonight," she said, "even if you did get me drunk."

"I had a lot of fun, too, even though I didn't."

Liz turned on the stereo, and we listened to an oldies station the rest of the way to her house. She turned her head just so that I couldn't tell whether she was asleep.

When we rolled through downtown, she wiped her puffy eyes and gave me directions to her place. We pulled in to a carport in front of her house, and I savored the subtle rumble of the car before I killed the engine and handed her the keys.

"So?"

"It's nice," I said. "Very nice."

"You bet it's nice. It's rad." She winked. "Let's go."

Liz lived in a beachfront townhouse that no one could afford on a reporter's salary, no matter how good she was. We walked up the whitewashed stairs to her door, Liz swinging her small set of keys around her finger like a party favor. She turned around to see if I was still behind her, and in doing so, the keys launched from her finger like a helicopter, flying into the air and then falling to the sidewalk underneath the stairs.

"Whoops!" she shouted.

"Don't worry, I'll get them." I was already making my way down the steps.

"Thanks." She slumped against the stucco wall next to her front door.

I walked underneath the stairs and fumbled for her keys in the dark. From the steps, I had seen where they landed, but in the darkness below, I was lost.

Liz leaned over the stairwell. "Did you find them? I have a little flashlight in my purse."

"I'm alright." I looked up at Liz from under the stairwell and inadvertently caught a glimpse underneath her skirt. I was fairly certain she wasn't wearing panties. Maybe Liz was too drunk to realize it, but she must have known the kind of view I had from below. Maybe she thought I wouldn't look, and so I felt bad for not doing otherwise. But I had to fight the urge to look again. I dropped to my knees and searched blindly for the keys. When my fingers finally found the tangle of metal, I lunged forward and grabbed them. I walked out from behind the stairs and threw the keys to Liz, but she didn't reach for them in time. They smacked the wall behind her.

"Nice shot, gunner."

"Sorry. Strong arm," I said.

Liz bent down for the keys and light twinkled off her cuff bracelet. She stood up and unlocked the door.

"Ready?"

I adjusted myself and walked up the stairs. "Ready."

The inside of Liz's house felt inviting. The walls were painted pale gray and trimmed with white molding. The wood floors were coated in a rich, dark stain. Matching silk pillows were neatly tucked in the corners of her leather couch and armchair. Abstract paintings hung from the walls. The pictures had earthy colors and thin, directional black lines, with scratched edges. They were large paintings, maybe five feet by eight feet, and they reminded me of California. A short pile of magazines, a tea cup and a pair of tortoise shell reading glasses were stacked messily on the ottoman. Light from the moon reflecting onto the ocean came through the window in her living room, guiding Liz as she clumsily palmed the wall in search of a switch. When she found it, she turned on the lights and walked into the kitchen past a wine fridge.

"That's a beauty," I said.

"This," she said, touching the fridge, "is my baby. There's a lot of my salary in here. You like wine?"

"Love it."

"Lets pop a cork then." Liz grabbed a wine opener with one hand and reached for a bottle with the other. She held it up in her hand like a trophy. "You like syrah?"

I nodded and made my way to her couch. Settling into the comfortable dark leather, I basked underneath the massive paintings while Liz tussled with the wine bottle in the kitchen. She brought the bottle and a pair of oversized crystal wineglasses into the living room. She placed the bottle and the glasses on a cherry coffee table that looked like it was from the 1920s, and poured wine into each glass. She took a sip from hers and waltzed across the room to the stereo, where she ran her fingers leisurely along the top row of her sprawling music collection. Much of it was vinyl, which immediately endeared her to me. I had left my albums in Wyoming—they were too hard to lug around. I missed them.

"Help yourself, Ethan," she said.

I picked up the glass. The rim engulfed my eyes and nose. I smelled the red wine inside and took a full drink. It tasted good. I wanted more. I wanted to catch up to Liz.

"What do you like?" Liz asked.

"Whatever." I reached for the bottle on the table and poured myself another glass. Liz rolled her head back in my direction and then crouched in front of a row of albums on the bottom shelf.

"The music critic has no preferences?" Her knees were locked together, and it was like she had now realized what I had seen earlier. "We are not amused."

I smiled. "I don't know what you have." I sat up to come over to where she was, wondering if this was the moment when a move should be made. Tabitha was never that playful, nor that seductive.

"Kick back." She motioned for me to stay seated. "Try me."

"Charlie Parker," I announced, wanting to exercise my musical expertise, but not wanting to come off showy. Jazz was a logical choice given the hour. I pondered Ornette Coleman, knowing it was a sly name to drop, knowing she wouldn't have any—nobody did.

"That's Sunday morning music, not late-on-a-school-night music."

"Good point," I said. "How about Miles?"

"There you go," she said, wiggling in her skirt as she

reached for a record from her collection. She put on "Birth of the Cool" and picked up her wine from the floor.

"So, what's your story, kid?" Liz asked as she sat next to me on the couch.

I picked up a Maceo Parker CD jewel case from the pile on the ottoman. "I've never heard this album," I said.

"Hey now. I told you all about my adulterous roots," she said, mischievously poking me in the ribs. I wondered if the humor, flirtatiousness and empathy were tactics she used on all her interviewees. "You work in newspapers. You're supposed to get this. Don't be so evasive."

"I'm not being evasive, not at all," I said, being evasive about my pressuring dad and joyless sex with Kristen and finding Indira. The only thing I ever wanted to share about my life with anyone was that I'd been cheated out of working at *Record Shelves*. And that was just for sympathy. "I already told you about my failed rock journalism career."

"What music is the rock journalist into? All kinds, I'd imagine."

"Well, in high school I did the grunge thing. Listened to Pearl Jam, wore flannels stolen out of my dad's closet."

"Cute," she said.

"Yeah. And then in college I got into a rockabilly-swing phase. I try to forget about that phase. I guess now I'm into a movie soundtrack phase, you know? Like Wes Anderson movies. I wear Wallabees, listen to The Kinks."

"When do you get into the Ethan Ames phase?" She

swished the wine in her glass.

"Very funny."

"No, really, I like Wallabees. Very college professor. Want me to be your naughty grad student? It's in my genes." She pinched my elbow and I began an erection. I crossed my leg, hoping she wouldn't notice. But I think she did.

"So why did you and Kristen split?"

"How do you even know about that?"

"Honey," she said—and it sounded much better than "kid"—"I know everything."

I looked down at my sneakers and took a deep breath. "Pour me some more wine."

I was half-awake at three or so in the morning when the heater kicked on, breaking the coastal chill of the house. The noise of the blowing air nearly drowned out the soothing calm of the waves crashing outside. I looked over and saw Liz in a black silk kimono, curled on her side, asleep in her armchair. Not where I had left her on the couch.

Right before I went back to sleep, I teased myself with a mirage of chasing Liz into the ocean, both of us naked, Indira watching from the sand.

7

Liz navigated morning traffic like she was her dad on an old Torrey Pines racetrack, the Speedster's engine firing like a pistol. It felt good to be in the Speedster again, all that cool, salty air blowing past my face. We were hung over, and we were tired. Liz kept her focus on the road in front of her. I watched the traffic behind us in the rearview mirror. I watched Liz shift into fourth out of the corner of my eye. Her hair was blowing straight back like a race flag in high wind.

She pulled up to the front office of the motel. The car, idling proudly among the parked hatchbacks and Ryder trucks, looked like a rich preppy kicked out of private school.

"So this is it?" Liz observed. She scrunched her lip to one corner of her mouth, warping the bottom half of her face. "Not exactly Shangri La."

"It's not so bad. At least it's not under a bridge."

Liz shook her head disapprovingly as I got out of the car.

"I have an idea. Stay with me until you score a place. I have to file from Fallbrook, so you'd have to walk or get a ride tonight. I know my place is kind of far from the paper, but I have a bike you could use starting tomorrow."

"That's really generous, but—"

"We'll work out the details later. Do you want me to take your things now?"

"No, that's alright. But Liz, I don't know if this is a good idea."

"Why? Because of Indira? I told you, it's not a big deal."

"Indira?" I worried I might have drunkenly revealed something the night before, but I had hoped it was only paranoia. Had I *really* told her? At that moment, I vowed to never drink again. My temples pounded in applause.

"Ah. You don't remember," she said.

"Not really."

"It's quite the tale. But listen, I'm super late." She was backing out of the lot. "We'll talk tonight."

"Liz!"

She braked, put the car in neutral, but left it running. Quickly and thoroughly, she filled me on what I had told her the night before, stopping every couple of sentences.

"You *really* don't remember any of this?"

"Bits and pieces."

"Lightweight."

There was a story that ran in the paper back home about a guy I went to elementary school with who died after he got drunk by himself on Christmas Eve. He was found the next morning by his parents, face-down on his couch, his body cold. I had always been afraid of getting that drunk; I made a point never to drink so hard that I couldn't remember what I did. But Liz had coaxed it out of me.

She said we were on our second bottle of Pacific Rim when I told her everything: Indira, the garbage bin, *Tight Horizons*, the fight with Kristen. All of it.

"We're going to find her!" Liz shouted over the rumble of the car.

"What?"

"That's what I told you last night. We're going to find her. Indira."

"Now Liz—"

"Don't worry, there are ways. It'll be fun." She waved and shifted into reverse. "See you at work."

I waved back at her as she tore out of the lot. When she was no longer visible on the street, I pulled the room key from my pocket.

Thankfully, the maids had not yet been by. I hung the Do-Not-Disturb sign on the outside door handle and grabbed the picture. I rolled it into a tight cylinder, wrapped a rubber band around it and dropped it into the garbage can.

I removed my shoes, socks and jeans and laid them all on the other bed. I took a lengthy shower, the steam transforming the room into a musty sauna. When I was finished, I wrapped a towel around my body and rummaged through my hockey bag for reasonably fresh clothes. When I was dressed, I began to pack. I did a second round of checks in the closet and under the bed. I reached under the bed and grabbed a woman's sock. It was a little dusty, but it had a sweet, grapefruit scent, like the citrus scents of a bath store. It was baby blue and navy, with a white flowery design embroidered on the ankle. The thread around the ankle was coming undone, the elastic stretched loose. It was a well-loved half of a favorite pair.

Tabitha wore similar socks when the weather cooled and she swapped her chino skirts and sandals for Levis and Doc Martens. She favored patterns of daisies, farm animals or blueberries. They were a colorful distraction when we were watching a movie or studying on her dorm room floor. I'd watch her toes wiggle in the socks, the cartoon cows swaying as they grazed on the white-nylon range.

I wondered how long the sock had been under the bed, whether its owner missed it, or if she even knew it was gone. Inexplicably, I threw it in my bag.

The only thing that remained in the room was what I had thrown away. The top of the rolled-up magazine page peaked out of the green canister. Was I really going to leave her there? Because of Liz, I thought I might. But the feeling didn't last long. For the second time, I rescued Indira from the garbage man. I unrolled the paper and flattened it against my chest as I walked into the bathroom. I hit the light and closed the door.

8

I thought Liz would be asleep by the time I got to her place, having covered the distance on foot. But when I arrived on her doorstep, she greeted me, a paintbrush in one hand and a key in the other. She handed it to me.

"No need to knock," she said, tucking it into my palm. A welcoming hug followed. She was wearing a white wife-beater and blue-jean overalls and smelled of linseed oil, turpentine and bubblegum. "Put it on your keychain, OK? Want a margarita? They're strawberry."

"Sounds awesome." I stepped inside and set my heavy bag by the door. I wiped a bead of sweat from my forehead and rubbed at a kink in my shoulder.

"You should have let me get your bag today, dummy." Liz rubbed my shoulder with her fingertips. I melted.

I looked at the wet painting on her easel while she fumbled in the kitchen. It reminded me of a farm at sunset. The top two thirds of the picture were a hunter green sky that blended into a grayish khaki as it neared the horizon, where a series of black lines divided two tones of brown turf. There was a half circle of orange to the right side of the horizon, and it pierced the green sky. On the left, a quarter orange circle dipped into the turf. It was painted loosely, and I could see the bold-color remnants of an older painting underneath.

It was like the others hung throughout her house, and it occurred to me that the paintings were not lavish purchases but her own work.

Liz returned with freshly blended margaritas. I slurped the top off the nearly overflowing glass and pointed to the paintings on the walls.

"So all these are yours?"

"Yes. Is that terrible?"

"Not at all. They're really good. I actually thought they were all paintings you had bought."

"I like to surround myself with the things that I've created," Liz said with a trace of shame. "You can't do that with a newspaper story, you know?"

"Now that would be pretentious."

"Ink smudges all over your hands," she added, having fun with the idea, "and then it gets on your walls." We both found this amusing, like it was an inside joke.

"How often do you paint?"

"Every night. At least every night I'm not getting smashed with some punk copy editor. Though I do like to drink—like that wasn't obvious—and paint." She took a gulp of melting margarita. "To me, painting is a lot like writing, or at least the way I write. Splashes of color here, technical lines there. Building up layers until it's perfect."

I pointed to the wet canvas on the easel. "That one's

really beautiful."

"You're sweet. It's actually upside down, though."

"Oh," I said, embarrassed. "I'm sorry."

She laughed. "No, no, that's OK. If it wasn't mine, I wouldn't have known, either. I have an artist friend in La Jolla who tells me to never be afraid of turning my work on its head. You know, literally. He said it's the only way to discover the imperfections. He says, 'If you can't see the imperfections, if you can't confront them and reconcile them, then you won't be able to tell beauty from a turd in the toilet.'"

"What's this one about?"

"Hmm, I don't know. I definitely feel a disconnect, a division, subdivisions ruining the landscape."

"You should call it, 'Orange County.'"

"Very clever, Ethan," Liz said with a toast, our glasses clinking. "It's no wonder they want you writing headlines."

She took the painting off the easel and, her arms stretched wide, carried it over to a stack of canvases on the other side of the room.

"Well," I said, rising from the couch, "I'm going to clean up and get out of your hair for a while. I don't want to get in your way my first night here."

She was barely hanging on to the large stretcher frame with her fingertips. "You're leaving?"

"Yeah. I thought you might like a little time to yourself."

"Ethan, if I wanted time to myself, I wouldn't have asked you to stay at my place. I'm not the philanthropist you may think I am." She brought another painting over to the easel. It wasn't quite as large, but the theme was the same. "Stay. Have a drink. Help me figure out what is wrong with this one."

"You don't mind?"

"I don't mind."

Liz wiped her hands with a crumpled pair of old boxer shorts hanging from the easel and then returned to the couch.

"And for the record," she said, poking my ribs, "this one *is* upside down."

"Got it."

Liz sipped at the slush on the bottom of her margarita glass and peered at the picture, chewing a chunk of ice. I positioned myself on the couch so that I could scrutinize the painting without Liz knowing that I was also studying her out of the corner of my eye.

"It's the black line, isn't it?" she asked. I didn't say anything. She took my silence as a yes. "You're right. It's too heavy."

The black lines reminded me of a story that ran in the paper around Christmas last year about a class of second graders that sent care packages to troops overseas. They included cookies, DVDs, hand-made Christmas cards and tree toppers constructed from toilet paper tubes, aluminum foil and yarn. In the three-column photo that ran above the story, several of the kids were posed with the items. A boy held one of the tree toppers, which was colored with black crayon, around the face, giving the angel an Amish beard. It was distinctly the kind of drawing that only a child would do. Every shape and contour was outlined in black, as though the definition would make it more the thing it was supposed to be.

"Want me to throw on some music?"

"That sounds good."

Liz put in The Breeders' *Last Splash* and then tore off into the kitchen. The blender whirred, and she returned with a clear plastic pitcher filled with her fusion of strawberries and alcohol. My glass was topped off, and the pitcher was left within reach.

I spent the rest of the night pretending to watch her paint, though I paid more attention to her backside, and probably not nearly as covertly as I drunkenly thought. In a repeat of the night before, I awoke on her couch, disoriented, alone; this time, Liz had found her way to bed. Groggily, I gazed at her painting. The thick black lines were gone, covered with oranges and reds, and some time after I'd passed out, she had applied thinner black lines in their place. I fell back asleep, a little more certain of my surroundings.

This routine continued for several days. Liz liked to drink, I wasn't one to argue.

"You know what you can do for me, Ethan?" she asked one night after paying for our most recent liquor run. I had yet to pay for a single thing, not liquor, not food, not rent.

"Anything." I meant it, though I might not have, had I known what was coming.

"Tell me more about Indira."

I rolled away from her on the couch.

"I don't want to go there," I sulked. "It's stupid."

I hadn't pulled the picture out of my hockey bag since I'd taken up residence at Liz's. Part of that was a lack of privacy, but I had a few hours alone during the day when I'd been tempted. But for whatever reason, I'd left it where it was, folded, hidden.

"I'm not going to make you, if that's what you mean," she said. "I'm not going to kick you out or anything. I just thought you'd like to share."

"It's embarrassing, that's all." I swallowed the last of my Pacifico, pulling the lime wedge out of the bottle. I gnawed on the sour pulp, my lips sealed with a pucker.

"Don't be embarrassed. I think it's sweet. I really do."

"Right, sweet. Do you want another beer?" I headed into the kitchen. Liz didn't say anything, so I repeated the offer. She declined.

"I'm going to bed." She walked into the bedroom and shut the door.

I stood in the kitchen, perturbed by the quid pro quo. I drank alone the rest of the night, listening repeatedly to The Breeders at a low volume, my ear against one speaker so as not to disturb her.

In the morning, Liz was gone. The only signs that she had been up and about were a half-finished mug of tea with lipstick stains on the rim and a plate of muffin crumbs on the kitchen counter. There was also a sticky note by the coffeemaker.

"The magazine is published by Milk-N-It Media," it read. "I've got their number. Martinis tonight?—*L*"

"Hey there, stud," Liz said, patting my back as I pulled out a barstool. "You got my note?"

"I did, I did. How did you do it?" I'd looked online and all I'd found was a couple of low-res cover images, but that was all. No reference to a publisher or even a website.

"I've got connections," she said, rolling an olive between her lips.

"So what do you think?"

"What do you mean, 'What do I think?'" She waved

an index finger at Greg, who was already en route with another martini. "I think this is a pretty good lead is what I think."

"What's the plan? I just call and ask for her or what?"

"How's your portfolio? You've got the *Record Shelves* stuff, right? What else?

"What's that got to do with—"

"You have an interview with Milk-N-It's publisher," she said, nudging me in the rib with her elbow. "His name's George Conroy. It's at his office in Santa Monica."

"An interview? What are you talking about?" I was exasperated. "I'm no porno star."

"No, we're well aware of that," she teased. "Lucky for you, you don't have to be. You're interviewing for a copywriting job."

"What? Copywriting? What?"

"A copywriting gig. Hey, it's writing, right? And you'll be working in an office, just like you do now."

"An office just like now, huh? Somehow, I doubt that."

"Use your imagination, kid. Think about it. A porn star is just like every other office worker out there, right?"

I stared at Liz blankly. Somehow I didn't think a porno star would consider herself an "office worker."

"Come on, Ethan," she prodded, "put yourself in her shoes. If you were Indira, wouldn't you want someone who could commiserate, someone who understands the joys and challenges of the industry, and by that I mean, someone who could leave it at the office?"

"I have no idea."

"Yes, you do. I think you've given this a great deal of thought, actually."

She was right. There was a short story in the pop culture section of the latest issue of *Record Shelves* about Mary Manner, a popular porno star, and her husband and on-screen film partner, Christopher Aspen. They had appeared in more than fifty films together since their wedding two years ago. They were fun to watch, too. Of course, the crux of the *Record Shelves* story was about their vicious divorce proceedings.

"I like my current job just fine."

"No, you don't," she laughed.

"No, I don't."

"So?"

"So."

"Just do it."

I sighed. "Why not?"

She whacked me on the back like the bouncer at the door. "Good boy. Now let's celebrate." She waved down Greg and had him pour shots of whiskey for the three of us.

"I must be crazy. This is crazy."

"Maybe. Maybe not." She reached for one of the glasses and raised it in the air. "To changing careers." She clinked her glass first with mine and then with Greg's.

"Cheers."

9

The first day of my internship at *Record Shelves*, I woke early. I showered and put on my favorite jeans—baggy and washed to a precise fade—a gray Pavement t-shirt and white Chuck Taylors I'd bought at the Foot Locker in Times Square the day before. For breakfast, I ate a bagel covered with lox, and I guzzled a pot of coffee while I read back issues of the magazine brought from home.

I caught an early train to Midtown, where the magazine's offices were located. Though it was early June, the air was hot and humid, and it turned the subway tunnel into a locker room-scented sauna. But I savored the experience, the rats crawling along the rails and then scattering when the train approached, the grimy concrete floors and the oily handrails. With my new pair of sneakers freshly scuffed from the subway and *Exile on Main Street* cranking on my iPod, I felt like one of The Ramones. All that was missing was the leather jacket.

The magazine's editorial offices were located in a skyscraper two blocks from Radio City Music Hall. A hallway of eight different elevators, each capable of scaling the building's ninety-two floors, divided the ground level into a large lobby on one side and a corporate bank in the office spaces on the other. There were long lines formed in front of the elevators, and while I waited, I listened to the chatter of Wall Street types in suits and slick hair speaking into their cell phones. Three women dressed in tight skirts, heels and turtleneck sweaters bantered about a new vegan make-up line while they sipped their Starbucks. When I finally stepped onto the elevator, I tingled with excitement, knowing that I would soon enter a world that had little in common with those standing beside me.

But *Record Shelves* wasn't much different. The other interns dressed like the editors, and the editors dressed like they were from The City, not like they were coming off a weekend bender at CBGB. They all wore variations on the same Banana Republic ensemble, black pants being the key feature. I was the only one dressed for a rock concert.

The *Record Shelves* office could have been an office anywhere, the corporate bank on the ground level or a software company in Silicon Valley. There were endless rows of cubicles, and every desk was outfitted with a flat-screen monitor, a black business card holder and a black iPod in a docking station. Bright fluorescent lights hummed overhead, and there was a faint odor of paper and new carpet that made the place smell like the Barnes & Noble near my dorm.

The life-size pictures of Jimi Hendrix, Janis Joplin and Keith Moon hanging from the walls, the "Sgt.

Peppers" projecting from slender Bose speakers perched over a table in a conference room, these were merely artifacts from a more raucous era, an advertisement for rock-and-roll credibility. The gelled hair and the tight skirts and the coffee cups with the cardboard sleeves were the new face of the magazine. Most of the editors at *Record Shelves* hadn't even honed their skills writing music reviews at free underground weeklies or hometown dailies. They were educated, pedigreed and handsome. They migrated to *Record Shelves* from the features desk at *Playboy* or the style section of *GQ.* One came from *Sports Illustrated.* Rarely, if ever, did I hear a spirited argument about the superiority of *Wowee Zowee* to *Slanted and Enchanted*, of *Ziggy Stardust* to *Aladdin Sane.* Typical discussions were about the Knicks' chances in the playoffs or securing dinner reservations at Del Posto.

One Wednesday, I arrived to find the staff frantically cleaning their desks, plowing whole piles of white paper with their arms into recycle bins next to their desks. I asked an editorial assistant—the lowest position one could have at the magazine without being an unpaid intern—what was going on. She told me that Marc Walker, the magazine's legendary founder and editor, was kind of a clean freak. Staffers were expected to keep their work areas tidy at all times, and he went so far as to conduct spot inspections twice a year, which, she said, were "brutal."

"Marc has a habit of doing it when we're on deadline for a double issue, of course. Like we don't have a million other things to be doing at the moment," she said, "besides scrubbing the coffee stains off our desk calendars."

Milk-N-It occupied an eccentric five-story building on Santa Monica Boulevard. A security guard behind a marble-top desk in the lobby checked a clipboard for my name and then escorted me to an elevator. He pushed a button for the fifth floor and instructed me to stay on it until I arrived.

"Don't go wandering," he warned. I nodded.

"I mean it."

"Got it," I replied as the doors closed.

After *Record Shelves*, I knew I wouldn't find anything shocking at Milk-N-It Media. There would be no posters of porno stars hanging on the walls, no rowdy editors arguing over which of Mary Manner's films was her best, no cheesy porno soundtrack playing in the background. I arrived at Milk-N-It Media with a good idea of how the publishing world worked, and it didn't work like that.

The elevator went right to the top floor. I stepped into an office space about the size of the newsroom. It was undergoing a renovation, though there were no construction workers to be found. Plastic partitions hung from the rafters. They rustled as I walked by, their frayed ends scraping along the bare cement floor. I parted a murky curtain and approached a reception desk. Though she was nearly camouflaged by the tarps and sawdust on the marble countertop in front of her, there was an older woman seated behind it,.

"I'm Ethan Ames. I have an appointment with Mr. Conroy."

She checked her computer against a hand-written schedule.

"I'll tell him you've arrived. Have a seat, please." She

pointed to a small waiting area across the hall.

I wiped a thin layer of white dust from a leather-bound armchair and thumbed through a pile of magazines splayed across a coffee table. There, among the tattered, year-old copies of *Sunset* and *ESPN*, was a shiny new copy of *Tittered*. Once the company's flagship publication, *Tittered* was said to have folded a year before, a victim of poor sales and the company's shifting focus to online-video distribution.

Why did I know this? Liz and I had spent the previous night surfing Milk-N-It's corporate website while we polished off a couple bottles of barbera.

"Always do your homework before an interview," Liz instructed.

"And always show up with a hangover," I teased.

Though Liz had seen the picture of Indira, our "research" on Milk-N-It was the first time I had viewed porno with her, the first time with any girl, actually. Kristen certainly wouldn't look at it, and neither would Tabitha. We clicked through "Milk-N-It Maidens," following links to the personal homepages of the company's stars. Then there was the "Hall of Came," a kind of greatest hits collection of Milk-N-It's best and brightest, posed in thumbnails that could be expanded into high-resolution jpegs with registration and a major credit card. Buzzed off the wine, Liz pulled her Visa from her purse, but I convinced her to put it back. After all, none of the thumbnails were of Indira. There was, in fact, not one reference to *Tight Horizons* on the site.

I eyeballed the copy of *Tittered* on the coffee table outside Conroy's office. I wanted to read it, but was I supposed to? I suspected a prank, that Ashton Kutcher was going to leap out from under the receptionist's desk at any second with a hand-held camera satellite-linked to my father's computer. But why would it be a prank? There were copies of *Record Shelves* in the magazine's waiting area. Why would Milk-N-It be any different?

"Mr. Conroy will see you now."

The receptionist was standing over me. She held a manila folder close to her chest like a schoolmarm guarding the answer key to a test.

I hadn't even reached for the magazine, only stared at the bare-chested woman on the cover, and already I was erect. I covered my lap with my bag and straightened my tie as though I had only ever worn a clip-on. I buttoned my coat as if everything else I owned was Velcro. I parted my hair with my fingers.

The receptionist was amused by my attempt to hide the obvious. She chuckled to herself, but not cruelly.

"That's fine, dear, take your time," she assured me. "If our work didn't have that effect on young men like yourself, we wouldn't be doing our job very well."

"Who, me? No," I said, keeping my bag in front of my groin as I rose, awkwardly. "I'm fine. I'm good."

"I see." She nodded and pointed down the hallway. "Shall we, then?"

"We shall."

Conroy's office reminded me of Marc Walker's. There was the black furniture and large windows that allowed for full natural light. His desk was a muted black slab of buffed concrete on a rounded chrome stand. Behind his black-leather office chair was a row of black lacquer cabinets and shelves.

George Conroy stared intently at a gratuitously large

widescreen television on the wall behind his desk, and he did not stop to look at us when we walked inside. He was watching a porno. The footage seemed raw, maybe from a recent shoot. He was studying a close-up of a woman's pubic region, as though he was counting every magnified pixel for fear of being shortchanged.

"Someone tell this girl to lose the colossal landing strip." He turned his head back toward the receptionist, as if she was the only one in the room. "Christ, I can't see her box through the goddamned thing."

The receptionist nodded obediently and then pointed me to a black director's chair in front of his desk.

"Have a seat here," she directed in a near whisper, as though she was worried Conroy might miss a critical juncture of dialog.

"It's more like a goddamned road block," he continued to himself.

She set the manila folder on the desk next to a black laptop and BlackBerry, the only other items on Conroy's desk. There were no coffee cups, pens, Wite-Out, desk calendars or other debris to indicate the work area of a laboring publisher. Conroy didn't have any framed photographs of friends or family on display. Not even a signed picture from a porno star.

"Would you like water?" the receptionist asked so softly, she could have been offering milk and cookies to a sleepless grandchild. "We have still and sparkling."

"I'm fine. But thank you," I said, clinging to the older woman with my eyes. I was drowning in the immense ocean of HD screen before me, the pulsating waves of breasts and orgasms, and her hospitality was a life preserver. "It's nice of you to offer," I gushed. "I really appreciate it."

"I know, dear."

The best day of my *Record Shelves* internship was the day I was given a research assignment for Marc Walker. I use "research" loosely, because it mostly consisted of photocopying old articles about the Rolling Stones and a few other boomer bands from the magazine's archives. Walker started *Record Shelves* as a college dropout in Los Angeles, and he'd written many of the first features. He was my idol, the guy who kept the faith for those of us who still gave a rip about rock-and-roll. I would have photocopied his underwear if they asked me. I definitely would have kept my desk clean—if they'd ever given me one.

After two days of photocopying, cutting, fastidiously organizing and assembling, I was ready to present Walker with the history of his magazine, a thick packet practically tied in a bow. Walker's assistant escorted me into his office to deliver the goods, and as I followed her through the greeting area of his office suite, I was feeling a renewed excitement about the place.

Inside, Walker, dressed in a dark suit, crisp white Oxford and a pink silk tie, talked fast on his hands-free and banged away on his keyboard, a fresh cup of cappuccino on a saucer at the ready. If I didn't know better, I would have thought he was transcribing—outside of fetching coffee, it was a standard-issue intern chore. His desk was devoid of clutter—not a paperweight or paperclip in sight, only his keyboard and a short stack of papers placed neatly on one end. The one small difference between Walker's office and a Scandinavian Designs show room was a framed photo of himself and Mick Jagger from the Seventies on a short bookshelf behind his desk. But even that had a showroom quality to it, with its cherry frame encasing the closely cropped black-and-white image. Were it not for Jagger's signature across the two men's chests, the photo could just as easily have been the glamour-shot placeholder found in department-store frames.

Walker told the person on the other end of the phone to hold. He smiled politely and accepted the package of articles. I didn't know what else I expected from the guy. He was obviously very busy, and I was only an intern. But I had daydreamed that he would rave about my clip packet, acknowledging the hard work and insight it had so obviously required. I pictured him inviting me to chat, and, dazzled by my institutional knowledge of the magazine, asking me how I knew so much about it.

But he didn't. The assistant escorted me from the office, and Walker resumed his phone interview, probably with some rock star blathering on the other end about musical influences and drug addictions, his every word diligently tapped into the computer. No tape for an intern to transcribe.

Conroy paused the screen and swiveled in his chair. The woman's spread legs on the screen behind his head were like bunny ears in a gag photo.

Though I hadn't expected to find a sharkskin-suited pimp straight out of a bad movie, I still thought Conroy would be older and maybe more worn-down by the stress of running such an operation. But he looked more like an Abercrombie and Fitch understudy. His face was thin and sculpted, and his short brown hair was articulated into a careful construction of manufactured bedhead. He wore a black designer safari shirt, the collar painstakingly rumpled, the cuffs and top three buttons undone, revealing his tanned, toned and hairless chest. His crisp designer jeans, a deep indigo, were nearly as dark as his shirt.

Conroy set the television remote on the desk and leaned back in his chair. He fiddled with his handheld and then reached for the folder on the desk. He read the contents inside.

"Ethan Ames, huh?" He kicked his feet up on the desk, showing off a new pair of black suede Vans. Conroy closed the folder and threw it back on the desk. I began to rummage through my bag for my clips, but he waved his hand in the air, uninterested in the formalities of reference letters and portfolios. I closed the bag and rested it on my lap, much like I had done in the waiting area.

He rubbed his hands together. "What kind of car do you drive, Ethan?"

It was an unexpected question and one of the few I hadn't practiced answering. I debated whether I should claim the Speedster as my own, but it just felt too dishonest, all things considered. I had driven it to Santa Monica at Liz's insistence. She had a light day at work, she said, and could ride her bike. Since I'd taken up residence at her house, Liz had become enamored with the idea that a person could get around in Southern California without a car. But somehow I doubted that my pedestrian lifestyle would impress a guy like Conroy.

"An Eighty-Nine Subaru," I answered, recalling the old car I had sold before I moved. I had inherited it from my dad on my sixteenth birthday, the same day he bought himself a new Outback. That wagon had been meticulously cared for by my dad, but that all changed when I took it over. By the time I dispatched it, for far less than what it would have been worth had it received proper attention, there were rust spots on the exterior and the obligatory rock chips in the front-end paint from the sanded roads of snowy Wyoming winters. Inside, the air vents were dislodged from the dashboard, shifting freely back and forth in the console. The tape deck no longer turned, the dome light was cracked, and there were numerous tears, scuffs and cigarette burns all over the upholstery. There wasn't anything inside of that car I hadn't managed to break or otherwise ruin. And yet, even with its ragged condition, the car ran like a tank, surviving everything a high school kid could put it through: cookies in ice-slicked parking lots, hot-dogging through snowdrifts, two-tracking over washboard-riddled dirt roads. I suddenly missed the car. It wasn't pretty, it never was, and I had only made it worse. But it was solid.

"Huh. I lease a Cayenne." Conroy spun around in his chair and looked out the window at the black SUV parked in front of the office. "Just got it today. This is a good business, guy. Why not drive something better?"

"It's paid for. It gets good mileage."

He laughed. "Mine don't."

"Yeah, well, Porsches are nice." I had the feeling he was fishing for something deeper. "I have a friend who owns an old 356. I say old, but it's in great shape."

"Coupe?"

"No, a Speedster."

"No shit? Original? That's a rare car."

"I think so. I'm told it was raced overseas."

"I'd like to meet this 'friend.' Unless it's a guy, in which case, I'm not gay."

"She's actually—"

"Not that there's anything wrong with that, being gay. Milk-N-It does very well in that segment. Those queers are horny, you know what I mean?"

"Actually—"

"I think it has something to do with how goddamned lonely they feel out there in America. 'Goddamned.' I used to be scared to say that, like I'd get struck down from heaven or something. But now I say it all the goddamned time, like I'm in some Salinger novel. Some people say 'motherfucker,' but 'motherfucker,' that's so, I don't know, it's so goddamned *Hollywood*, you know? Like it makes you sound tough, whereas otherwise you're just some dumb fag acting in one of my films instead of that Hollywood blockbuster you told your folks about. Way to go, Mr. Curtis Goddamn Seinfeld, or whatever the hell your name is. You made it. Welcome to L.A., *motherfucker*."

He lit a Marlboro Red. "So who's this friend of yours with the Speedster?"

"I think you know her, Elizabeth Anderson Carlisle?"

"No shit, Liz owns a Speedster?" he asked. "Sure I know Liz. Not in the goddamned Biblical sense, or anything, if you know what I mean." He stared at me with suspicion until I acknowledged with a nod that I knew what he meant.

He puffed on the cigarette twice and then put it out, even though it had only just begun to smolder. "So tell me about yourself, guy. You're looking for a job? Here's what I want to know: Where do you see Milk-N-It going? In fact, where is this whole goddamned industry going? First there was *Playboy*, then there was *Hustler*, and then, of course, video, and then the Internet, and then goddamned Voracious changes everything, hiring those goddamned babes—a few of which I *have* had Bible studies with, if you feel me."

Everybody knew about Voracious, even my dad, who bellyached about the Associated Press's obsession with covering the company and its effect on the entertainment industry. "They expect me to run that kind of story in a family-owned newspaper?" he whined. Voracious was the largest-grossing producer of adult entertainment, and was widely credited with making "porn star" part of the country's vernacular. They hired attractive girls, filmed only heterosexual scenes and distributed their films to any hotel with Pay-Per-View, right alongside the video games for the kids. The owners were swimming in profits. They lobbied Congress. They branched out into mainstream movie-making. They sponsored NASCAR.

"What I would like to know," he said, browsing the contents of the folder again, "Ethan Ames, is how *you* can help me take it to the next goddamned level." He waited for a reply, and not patiently.

"Well, the newspaper where I work just ran a story on how porno is becoming more mainstream."

"That's true."

"But I think for the couple that watches one movie a year, like in a hotel room or on Valentine's Day or whatever, some of the stuff in a porno might be a turnoff."

"Such as?"

"Well, it would be cool to feature prettier girls."

"Prettier girls, huh? You're thinking of Voracious now. Let me tell you, there aren't a lot of 'prettier girls' who will let you film them sucking dick. And the ones that are out there require quite a goddamned fee. Most of the time it's more than what I make on a single goddamned movie."

"Of course," I offered, like it was a well-known fact that had momentarily slipped my mind.

"There's also the matter of cum shots," I countered. The words surprised Conroy. They surprised me.

"Yes, there's always the matter of cum shots," he laughed. "What about them?"

"I don't know. I guess it's like watching someone hock a loogie into someone's mouth. I mean, I like it. But it's kind of nasty, too."

He slapped the desk with his palm. "Ha! What a business we're in, Ames. Listen, I get what you're saying, but I don't agree. The freaks eat up the slurpy stuff. I've got the goddamned numbers to prove it. But I like the way you think. You've got vision. So here's what I'm going to do."

Conroy grabbed his hand-held and typed furiously with his thumbs.

"I've just instructed that lovely lady out there, Lorraine, to set you up for the trial run. She'll tell you all you need to know."

He threw the BlackBerry back on the desk like it was a half-eaten piece of pizza.

"Now get out of here, goddamn it." He grinned and winked at me like I was the apple of his eye. "You make me sick."

10

"Come on, man, I need details. I'm a reporter, babe. Gotta know." Liz sat eagerly on the couch, still in her work clothes. She had just barely beaten me home.

I took out the DVDs Lorraine had given me per Conroy's instructions and spread them on the floor. They were nearly identical in their black cases, each covered with scratched plastic sheeting. The discs inside were covered with black labels, hiding the old labels underneath. They were numbered one through five with a white paint marker.

Lorraine told me the discs featured films that were no longer in circulation. They depicted various genres, from bisexual to barely legal. Lorraine said I wouldn't find any information about the films online, and unless I was an extreme porno junkie, she assured me, I wouldn't recognize any of the players, either.

"They want me to do a trial run."

"Really?" Liz asked. "And those are the trial run?"

"Yes."

"That's a lot of porn."

"I don't have to watch them all."

Lorraine said I should pick three to write about. It would give them an idea of my strengths, she said, and also my interests. I was to provide movie titles, subtitles, two hundred words of marketing copy for each and suggestions for images (with captions) to be used on the back covers.

"'Have to,' huh? Good of you to limit yourself." Liz examined the pile further. "Do you get to keep them when you're done?"

"No." I produced the prepaid FedEx envelope Lorraine had given me.

"Oh how cheap."

"Of course," I said, "with this, I could buy twenty new ones." I handed her the check Lorraine gave me from my back pocket. It was for five hundred dollars.

"Conroy certainly is a big spender." Liz shook her head.

"I know. The most *Record Shelves* ever paid me was half that."

"Well, don't get too excited."

"About the money? But it is exciting. I earn this in a week at the paper."

"You just want to be careful. With Conroy."

"What do you mean? Do you think this was a bad idea?" I wanted to remind Liz that it was *her* idea.

"No, I don't. Just remember who you're dealing with."

"And who's that?"

"A con man, of course."

"He's slick, yeah, I'll give you that."

"Slick isn't the half of it."

Liz picked up one of the cases, handling it like an ancient artifact. She tapped it against her palm. "He sells people lies."

"And he makes a lot of money doing it," I said. "Nothing wrong with that. Have you seen his office? His big ass TV?"

"No," she said, running her fingers over the black-faced disc inside like she was reading Braille, "I haven't."

"I guess I assumed you had."

"What's that supposed to mean?"

"Nothing." I looked at the case in her hand, and then the others on the floor. "You still think he can help with Indira, right? Otherwise, I mean, I'm risking a lot here."

She thought about it. "He'll get us closer, I think."

Us, she said. I liked that. We were a team.

"But you'd better do a good job. George Conroy's not easily impressed."

"Then I assume you'll have no problem writing all of this for me, right?"

"I will do no such thing." Liz opened the case and removed the DVD. She flung it at me like a Frisbee. "But I see no reason why I can't help." She winked. "Put that in. I'll be right back."

Liz changed into faded jeans and a tight v-neck. She went into the kitchen and returned with a bottle of red wine and two glasses. I held them while she worked at pulling the cork. When the wine was poured, Liz sat on the opposite end of the small couch and put her bare feet on the ottoman. Her toenails were painted bright red.

"Start it up," Liz commanded unceremoniously.

I put the DVD into the player and returned to the couch. Liz held the glass to her nose, sniffed its contents and took a swig. She threw the cork into the kitchen, almost missing the sink.

"You're going to be fine," she said, sensing my discomfort. "Think of it like a music review."

I grabbed the remote and turned on the TV. There were no root menus, no chapters. The DVD launched right into action. I put the remotes back on the end table and shifted in my seat. "Easier said than done."

"I know." She playfully belted me across the chest with one of the pillows on the couch. "Make yourself comfortable."

An hour had passed before the movie swelled into a hetero orgy, the finale, and I wasn't sorry to see it end. Not that it was a bad movie. Under different circumstances, I might have enjoyed it. But I'd spent most of the time acting the nervous teenager, mocking the silly dialog or the sloppy appearance of a microphone in the movie frame. Liz, in contrast, spoke little, and only seriously, as though she was a critic at a foreign film festival. She wondered why some actors wore condoms while others didn't, why some shaved and others didn't, whether tattoos made them more desirable or less.

Liz grabbed the pillow I had tucked under my arm for privacy and put her head on my lap before I could stop her. I adjusted myself, hoping she wouldn't notice, knowing that of course she would. Liz bunched the pillow under her arm and stretched her legs across the couch. "That's much more comfortable. Do you mind?"

"Not at all." Except there was nowhere for my right

arm to go except on top of her outstretched leg, and I did so tentatively, keeping it at a near-hover over her body until I could hold it no longer. She nestled into my side, practically purring as she did so.

"Are we giving this one a thumbs up, Mr. Ebert?"

"I suppose so. It's been pretty good. I can say that, right?"

"Yes, stud, you can say that." Liz glanced at me. "You haven't heard me complaining."

She stretched her body, putting an arm across my lap, her hand rested on my knee. She rubbed her feet together, slowly. "My toes are cold."

I pulled the *serape* off the back of the couch and bunched it over her feet. This time, I didn't deliberate. I rested my arm on her hip, my hand slowly closing around the top of her thigh.

When the DVD ended, Liz reached over my lap, grabbed the remote from the end table and started it over. Before I knew it, we were kissing, Conroy's cheap film playing in the background like an instructional video, the sounds that projected from the TV blending with our own.

I woke up alone on the couch, covered in the *serape*. I called out to Liz, but I had a pretty good feeling that she was gone. I threw the blanket to the floor and got up, walking past the DVDs still stacked near the TV on my way to the bathroom. I wondered if I needed them anymore.

I put on clothes and went into the kitchen. Usually Liz left me a note near the coffeemaker to wish me good morning or inform me that there was coffee in the Thermos, that she would be having a late night at work and so she could give me a ride home. But there was no note. There was no coffee.

I poured water into the coffeemaker and put French roast in the grinder. I dumped bread in the toaster. I lowered my mouth under the faucet and slurped a gulp of running water while my caffeine percolated. I crunched my toast and drank my coffee. When I finished, I put the plate and cup in the dishwasher and returned to the table with a legal pad from my bag. I jotted down ideas from last night's movie. When I was done, I went to the living room and put in a new DVD.

And then another.

And another.

And finally, the last of the five, disregarding Lorraine's instructions. Call it extra credit.

When it was all over, I was sprinting to work, unshaven, unshowered and wearing yesterday's boxers. I had watched four films, masturbated twice and filled a reporter's notebook full of copy.

It was my best writing yet.

11

"You've got what it takes, guy," he said. There was a rustle of paper, and then Conroy cleared his throat. "'When kinky Consuela aches to give her cowboy head, Pete slings his skin pistol into her mouth and pumps that *bandita* full of lead.' Brilliant. Really goddamned brilliant."

"Thanks, Mr. Conroy." I whispered into my cell phone as I hurried out of the newsroom. Liz caught my eye as I rushed out the door, the first time we had acknowledged each other since the night before.

"They won't think we're talking about shooting somebody, right?" he asked.

"I don't think so. The pictures help make the connection." I figured if it worked for newspapers, it must work for the cover of a porno.

"Because there's a goddamned market for that stuff, if you can believe it. Milk-N-It doesn't go there, but there is a market. Sick bastards. They'll strangle these chicks, hit 'em, practically rape 'em. In fact, I think they do rape 'em. Christ, it's bizarre."

"I had no idea."

"I would go there, don't get me wrong, I like to make a goddamned buck. But not in the horror show, the sick bastards. Anyway, you're in. There's a shoot on Friday I want you at. The script needs banged into shape. Because right now, it's lousy. Goddamned lousy."

That was only three days away, and Friday was the busiest day of the week. Weekend-package layouts, advanced pages, the bulk of the bulldog, and all on top of the next day's edition. No day was a good day to leave a newspaper—ask my dad, ask my editor—but Friday was an especially bad day to leave. And yet that was a peripheral concern to the larger one looping in my head, and in my father's voice. Was I really going to quit newspapers to work in adult entertainment? I could see the hand-wringing editorials now.

"It's a little soon," I told George. I scanned the darkened windows of the newsroom from the other side of the parking lot. I turned back toward the row of oak trees that separated the newspaper from the highway.

"I've got another guy I can go with. I've got this goddamned shoot, and it's critical I get someone in there who knows what to do with a few words. But, look, if you're not interested—"

"I'll do it." I swallowed hard.

"Great. Friday at one. It's on Gilmore in Van Nuys, near the golf course. Call Lorraine if you have questions. You won't miss it."

"I'm sure I'll find it."

"I meant the job, the goddamned newspaper job. You won't miss it a bit. No more beating off at a desk.

You're in the big time now, guy. You're in pictures." And he hung up.

I folded my cell phone into my pocket and kicked a rock across the parking lot. Liz stood outside, hands raised tentatively in the air like a referee unsure about a field goal. I gave her a thumbs-up.

"He wants me to start Friday," I said as I walked toward her. "Look, Liz, about last night."

"What about it?" she asked casually, as though we had stayed up late watching cable news and eating ice cream.

"What about us?"

"What do you mean, Ethan? We'll still hang out."

Then she paused for further consideration. "Wait," she continued, "I know what you mean. You can stay at my place still. That is, as long as you don't mind the commute?"

"No, I don't mind," I answered. "I guess I better buy a car though. Think I can find an old Subaru for cheap?" I should never have gotten rid of mine. It was dumb to think I could survive without a car out here.

Liz plopped the keys in my hand.

"Just get me home tonight."

"Liz, I can't take your car. You need it."

"I'll get by."

"What are you going to do?" I sounded whiny.

"I'll get by. So it's settled then?"

"It's settled. Listen, I really appreciate—"

"C'mon. Let's go tell everyone our boy's hit the big time." She grabbed my arm and marched me toward the newsroom. "Let's go tell them Ethan Ames is in pictures now."

12

Traffic thickened near L.A. and ground to a halt just past Torrance. To pass the time, I played my favorite game, looking for hints of Indira through the windows of cars in front of me. A girl in a Beetle had Indira's blonde hair, pulled into a ponytail. I saw Indira's profile in a mother reaching to the backseat to help an infant in a car seat. The girl in the Jeep wore a black sports watch around her wrist, which I thought made sense. Indira would have to be athletic to maintain that figure.

I exited the freeway and navigated my way through a maze of dilapidated housing to the west side of Van Nuys and drove into a cul-de-sac in a nice neighborhood. The lawns were lush and well-groomed. Each porch was sprinkled with colorful potted plants. Kids played in the street.

I pulled in front of a two-story stucco home with the address from Lorraine. There was a black luxury SUV parked diagonally on the front lawn. A mix of sporty coupes and banged-up light trucks sandwiched on the driveway and along the street. The house stuck out in comparison to the others, though exactly how, I couldn't say. Like its neighbors, its suburban façade was well maintained, with its homeowners association paint job and matching mailbox. There was nothing about it—save the poorly parked SUV, perhaps—that indicated there was anything different about the house and its inhabitants. And maybe that was just it. Maybe the place looked *too* normal. Maybe it was because I knew what lurked inside.

I parked in front of a house on the other side of the cul-de-sac. A woman in her late sixties stood on the front porch, watching me suspiciously, a hand stretched above her eyes to block the sun. I killed the engine and opened the door. She shook her head slowly back and forth, her face locked in a frown. I gave her a friendly smile, but either she didn't notice or didn't care. She continued to watch the activities across the street, her lip curled, her face a tightened knot.

I turned around to see what she was looking at, and I saw a woman standing behind the fence alongside Conroy's place, her platinum blond hair bunched wildly over her head. She was staring toward the ground, a few heavy locks draped around her face and over her ears. Though she was partially obscured by the fence, from our angle, which was slightly elevated, we saw enough. She wore a blue terry cloth robe, which had come undone at her chest, exposing a breast. It was so large that even at our distance I could see the purple-pink of her nipple. The blond saw that we were watching. Quickly, she adjusted the robe and tightened the belt. Then she kneeled down, disappearing behind the fence.

A beat up Ford Ranger pulled in behind the Speed-ster. A guy in a white t-shirt, madras shorts and beige work boots got out of the truck. Both of his ears were pierced. His brown arms were covered with dark green tattoos.

"Nice ride, holmes," he said, eyeballing the car.

"Thanks."

He grabbed a tripod and lights from the truck bed, tipped the brim of his Dodgers hat toward the woman on the porch behind me and looked both ways before crossing the street.

I stood motionless, overcome by a surge of excite-ment and nerves. It felt like the first time I interviewed a big-name act for *Record Shelves*. I took a breath, swal-lowed and put a foot forward, followed by the other. I didn't look back at the irritated old woman behind me. I didn't look both ways when I crossed the street. I just moved before I figured out how to stop myself.

The equipment guy waited at the front door for some-one to let him in. His muscles were flexed, and his right bicep was covered with a large gauze bandage.

"Is this the shoot?" I asked congenially.

He turned around, nearly smacking me in the face with the bulky tri-pod perched on his shoulder. He studied me slowly and then nodded his head. He put his tri-pod down, rested it against his leg, and pressed the doorbell. A woman in a green silk kimono robe answered.

"Where's Franklin?" the equipment guy asked. "I need to get him this stuff."

"He's in the back, near the gate," she said matter-of-factly. "You better hurry. They're about to start."

The conversation was like one between a delivery-man asking a store clerk where she wanted her order unloaded. He moved past her, and she shifted her focus to me. She stood expectantly, awaiting an introduction. Maybe she thought I was there by mistake.

"I'm Ethan Ames." I shifted my weight from my heels to my toes as I extended my hand. She shook it suspiciously. I stepped back to steady myself, fairly certain I had just met my first real-life porno star. "George Conroy requested my services."

"Your services?" She thought about it like it was high school trigonometry. "Your services," she repeated.

"I'm here to help with the script. Is he around?"

"The script?"

Was there some secret knock I was supposed to know? Was the equipment guy, peering at me as he assembled his equipment in the foyer, going to throttle me if I didn't answer correctly?

"Is George around?"

"Oh, sweetie," she said like an older sister, "George doesn't come to these things."

"I had the impression he did."

"I think he's at the spa. It's Tuesday, right?" She checked her wrist, though she wasn't wearing a watch. It was, of course, Friday. I should have been at the newspaper. It felt like weeks since I had quit. But it had only been three days. "I think it's Tuesday. He's at the spa."

"Right. Well, George sent me. Can I come in?"

She stepped back into the shadow cast by the doorway and reached over to a narrow table along the wall in the foyer. She gave herself a quick look in the mirror, fixed a wisp of hair stuck to her mascara-coated eyelashes and brought a clipboard back to the doorway.

"Amos, you said?"

"Ames."

"Here you are, sweetie." She marked my name on a sheet attached to the clipboard with a red Sharpie. "Is this your first time?"

"Not at all." I certainly didn't want to admit to being a first-timer. Not to her.

"Then you know what to do." She extended her arm toward the back of the house. If I had wanted to turn back, it was too late now. I walked inside. She closed the door behind me and directed me to the sliding doors leading to the back yard.

"This is where we're doing most of the shoot today. That's the craft service table if you get hungry. There's a full bath upstairs, but they're using it, so you'll need to use the quarter bath down the hall." It was like touring the set of a sitcom.

"Thanks. I'm lucky to have such a helpful guide," I said, looking to charm her. I turned to see if she found me amusing. She certainly was smiling, but I don't think it was because of anything I had said.

"I'm stretching my mouth," my guide said in a far too perky manner. She had removed her robe and hung it on the coat rack near the breakfast nook. I stared at her breasts. And then my eyes sunk like an anchor.

"Sorry," I said, turning around as though I had accidently walked in on someone's dressing room. She giggled and teasingly tapped me on the shoulder.

"Go ahead and look." She placed her left foot behind her right, put one hand on her hips and threw the other in the air like one of the models from the "Price is Right." She had a tan line around her breasts. Her nipples were pierced. Her pubic area was perfectly sculpted, not a stray hair in the bunch. I stiffened and stuffed my hands deep into my pockets.

"That's what I'm here for!" She stared at my crotch.

"Very nice," I said, squirming. "You don't see something like that every day, do you?"

"You do if you've done this before." She unlocked her pose and walked past me, her ass swinging. It was hard to tell whether a porno star was being sarcastic.

I followed her through the sliding doorway. She took me to a wet bar on the patio and asked whether I wanted a cranberry and soda or a Red Bull.

"George has a strict policy against drinking on his sets," she said routinely. "Right, Avery?"

The bartender, dressed in a white button down and black slacks, held his hands behind his back and nodded in agreement. I told her it was no problem, greeted Avery and asked for a bottle of water.

"OK, good luck. Gotta go to work now." She walked across the yard, which was one large set, and toward a palm tree in a corner. She put her arm around a tall naked guy standing in leather flip flops and whispered something into his ear. Both of them waved at me and laughed. He had the biggest penis I had ever seen. It waved along with him.

"Sure you don't have any beer back there?" I asked Avery.

"Sorry, sir."

I turned back toward the couple, but they had already forgotten me. How did I know they had forgotten me? Because the lights surrounding them were brighter than a baseball field at night and she had his big, waving penis in her mouth.

A small camera crew gathered around my guide and her companion. I followed, and when I approached the scene, I heard the unmistakable sound of a blowjob. A slim guy in a loose gray t-shirt, black capri pants and sandals barked instructions. He slicked back his oily, dark hair and adjusted his headset. Judging from his reaction, my guide was doing the job just right.

Watching her give someone head, watching the crew watch her give head, I thought about how far I had drifted from the journalism career I envisioned for myself or, for that matter, the one my dad envisioned for me. If he thought a career at *Record Shelves* would have kept me from the editor's chair, I couldn't imagine what he would think of me standing at a porno shoot. I hadn't told him I'd quit the paper. We didn't talk much, so at least I wouldn't have to lie.

I looked to the crew for instructions, but they were busy working their cameras, adjusting lights and holding microphones. I pulled a pen and a legal pad from my bag and started to scribble. The director walked toward me, put his diminutive hands on my shoulders and moved me closer to the circle.

Quietly, I asked him where the script was, that Conroy had sent me to revise it. He chuckled to himself.

"Script is done. Do not worry."

"But Conroy told me to help out."

"You are copywriter? Write your copy. Don't worry about script. Mr. Conroy does not understand. Script is done." Then he shouted at my guide for "more spit, more phlegm."

A redheaded actor arrived on the scene, and my guide

switched to him while the first actor went behind her. I recorded every detail, careful not to let any action elude me. Frantically, I filled two pages with dialog, with moans, groans and slurping noises, all freakishly audible from where I stood. In the back of my mind, I wondered what Liz might think of my notes if she saw them. I had to remind myself, though, that this was her idea.

Without much notice, the two actors climaxed, using my guide as a target. The director called for a fifteen-minute break, and the crew busily moved their equipment to another corner of the yard, where a lesbian trio awaited their cue. The male actors patted their faces with hand towels and complimented each other's work. My guide stayed on the ground, and the two actors thanked her as they headed for the house, naked. A chubby assistant wearing skinny jeans, suede Vans and blue latex gloves waited until the last of the crewmembers had dispersed before she systematically wiped the actress's face, chest and hands with a hand towel. Awkwardly, I scribbled on my legal pad from afar, completely incapacitated and forced into a crouch. I had more notes than I would ever need, but it was all I could do. I couldn't stand up.

"What did you think, Mr. Film Critic?" my guide asked. "Did I get the Oscar?" She touched her lip, looked at her fingertips and then wiped them on the beach towel.

"I think you stole the show."

"Me, too." She threw her head back and her long hair fell on the towel. I was worried she might get something in it. Quietly, she repeated to herself, "Me, too."

13

The assistant helped my guide with her silk robe, and after they both left, I was safe to stand up and adjust myself. I scanned the expansive lawn, unsure where to go next. I saw the equipment guy from before come around the side of the house and head for the bar. He took a can of Coke from Avery and pushed away the accompanying glass of ice with a lime wedge on the rim. I swung my bag over my shoulder and followed him into the house, my notebook at the ready.

"Hey," I said when I caught up, "could you tell me where the next shoot is?"

He looked me over, his brows furled. "There's a reshoot upstairs. Dude came early."

"When does that start?" I asked.

"I don't know, man. I guess they going over lines now while he works up his bone. Who are you?"

"I'm Ethan Ames. The copywriter."

"Copywriter? Yeah, I don't know what the fuck that is," he said. I began to explain, but he interrupted. "You need something?"

"No. Sorry, I'm just new here," I said, offering my hand, "and I saw you outside."

He shook it. "'Sup man, I'm Eddie."

I followed him to the food table. Eddie set down his Coke and bit into a doughnut. He chewed with strong jaws, red jelly dangling from his lips, his mouth encircled by a ring of powdered sugar. Eddie took an oversized bite, threw the remainder on the table and grabbed a cocktail napkin to wipe his mouth. He crumpled it in his fist and threw it next to the doughnut. Then he reached for his equipment.

"Later, man."

"Are you going up there now?" I asked.

"Nah. I'm gonna have a smoke before I hit it."

"Could I come?"

"You smoke?" he asked.

"Occasionally."

"Alright, if you want."

I deliberated over whether I would actually smoke as we headed outside, but before I could make up my mind, Eddie offered and I accepted. He then produced a silver-plated lighter out of his pocket, lit his smoke first and mine second. I took a long pull. The smoke had a hollow, cardboard taste to it. I blew out the smoke and coughed. A little embarrassed, I pointed to the gauze on Eddie's arm. "You alright? That looks like a pretty major wound."

"Nah, man. That's my new tat." He patted the bandage tenderly.

"Can I see it?"

Eddie popped his cigarette into his mouth and peeled back the bandage. A square of dirty adhesive residue from the white surgical tape surrounding the gauze framed a tattoo of a crown of thorns floating over a crucifix. A swirl of ink wrapped around the cross turned into a banner with the name "Eddie Junior" inscribed in cursive. His skin was red and swollen underneath.

"My son," Eddie said.

"How many kids do you have?"

"Just the one."

"You're married?" I asked.

"Dude, you want the story of my life or what?"

"Just making conversation."

I neglected my cigarette, and a long ash fell on my shoe. I flicked it onto the ground.

"So how'd a dude like you end up working a job like this?" Eddie asked. "You go to college for this shit now?"

"No, you can't," I laughed. "I kind of stumbled into it, I guess. I used to work in newspapers."

"Why'd you leave a newspaper for this shit? That's straight work, man."

"It just didn't work out."

"What," he laughed, "you get fired?"

"No," I replied tersely. "It just didn't work out," I didn't know if it was safe yet to discuss Indira.

"Relax, holmes, I'm just kidding. Man, white boys is uptight."

Eddie kept an eye on the lady across the street. She was still pacing her porch.

"You know what, dude? That lady is gonna bust this show one of these days. I don't even know why they do this here. Neighbors get so pissed. Just rent a fucking studio or something. But Conroy, man, he's cheap."

"It does seem weird to make pornos in such a nice neighborhood."

"Pornos," he laughed. "Yeah, whatever. This is George's joint. He does whatever the fuck he wants."

"I guess," I said. "So you know Conroy?"

"Yeah."

"You like him?"

"Sure, whatever," Eddie said. He threw his cigarette onto the ground and stamped it out. "I got to get back in there. You should come, man. Dude may blow his load early every once in a while, but Big Bang Bob and Cherry Lollipop is some of the best."

I hadn't finished my cigarette, but I threw it on the ground. "Actually, I wondered if you could help me." I took a deep breath.

Eddie took his hand off the door handle. "Oh, yeah?"

"I'm looking for someone."

"Who's that?"

"A girl."

"I know a lot of girls, man. Who?"

"Her name's Indira. At least I think that's her name. She's, um..."

"She's what?"

"She's one of George's girls."

"His girls?"

"Yeah, his girls. You know, one of them." I pointed to the door.

He slapped his hands together and hunched over laughing. "One of *George's* girls. Got you, man. Indira, huh? Sorry, never heard of her."

"Never mind," I said.

"Sorry, man. Didn't realize you was serious."

The door swung open and a guy from another crew appeared. "Eddie, *vamonos*, gotta go," he said.

"Cool." Eddie turned back to me. "Sorry, dude. Wish I knew her. See you upstairs?"

"Wait." I unzipped the flap of my messenger bag and pulled out the picture of Indira, the edges slightly worn and curled. It was like I had pulled out the fluorescent pink missing poster that Chuck the motel clerk had made for Bethany. Eddie snatched the paper out of my hand and studied it.

"Nah, never seen her. You?" He handed it back to the waiting crewman.

"No, don't," I tried to object, but it was too late.

Eddie asked him. Then he turned back to me. "Carl's worked here a long time."

"Since the beginning," Carl said. He looked at the picture with a grimace. "Shit. We were kinda low-class back then." He shook his head, like he was looking over an old yearbook and couldn't believe how much weight he'd gained since high school.

"You recognize her?"

"No, she don't look familiar. Sometimes we'd hire these girls for just one gig, you know, then put 'em back on the street. Sorry, kid." He handed me the picture. "Eddie, *vamonos*."

"I gotta get back, dude," Eddie said.

"Yeah, go, forget it."

"Alright. Late."

I stayed outside to ponder Indira. When I entered the foyer, my tour guide arrived, having heard the front door open.

"Oh," she said, "just you." She tightened the belt on her robe, pivoted on one foot and headed back to wher-

ever she had come from. "Hope you're enjoying the
show."

14

I attended a shoot about once a week, working out a schedule with Liz so I could take her car to locations throughout L.A. I'd take notes, offer script suggestions and try hard not to walk around with a permanent erection. I thought after working for a few weeks that the embarrassing moments would go away, but they didn't. They were almost worse.

Occasionally, Eddie worked the same shoots as me, and if the timing was right, we convened for a cigarette break and an update on Indira. He gave me the signal, a slow nod, from across the room, and then put his camera in a corner of the living room of the ranch-style house where we were shooting. I had no idea where Conroy came up with the locations, but the one thing they all had in common was a nosy neighbor or two standing out on the street, watching the varied activities of a porno crew.

"So," he said, taking a drag and then pointing his cigarette at my chest, "any luck finding your girl?"

"Not really. I don't know what to do. I thought I might ask Conroy." I didn't, really, but it was an explanation. Why else was I standing on the porch of a porno shoot? I was there to find Indira, lest I forgot.

"Yeah, maybe."

"You don't think that's a good idea?"

"Maybe."

"Eddie, tell me."

"I don't know, dude." He took another drag and pointed at the Speedster, which was parked two houses down. "How's the mileage on that thing?"

"Pretty good, I guess." I was embarrassed that I had no idea, that I didn't pay attention to those things when I drove, only to the Indira in every lane.

"It's a nice ride," he said. Eddie was fishing, and we both knew it.

"We'll have to go for a ride some time."

"That'd be sweet, dude. What are you doing after work?"

"Nothing, I guess."

"Listen, man. You give me a ride in that thing, I'll make it worth it."

I pulled on the cigarette he had bummed me and gestured. "I probably owe you just for all the smokes."

"Alright. How's about it? You let me drive it, tonight," he said, "and we call it even."

"Oh, well, I don't know, Eddie..."

"See, I was thinking something."

"Yeah?"

"Yeah. I was thinking we should take that ride of yours to Santa Monica."

"Santa Monica?" We were in east L.A.

"Yeah, man. See, I was thinking, Conroy got files on

all his girls. You know what I'm saying?"

"On Indira?" I asked, encouraged. "What's in the files?"

"All kinds of shit. Applications, credit checks, copies of their drivers licenses. Probably photos. It's for the government, in case they ever raid the joint. They want proof the models are healthy and eighteen, know what I'm saying? They don't want no pedophiles."

"Of course."

"We could sneak a peak. It'd be after hours, but that ain't no problem." Eddie reached into his pocket and produced keys to the office. I didn't ask how he got them. I didn't want to know. I didn't even have one key to Milk-N-It, let alone several.

"But, wait, won't Conroy be pissed?"

"Probably. That a problem?"

There was a story in the newspaper about a janitor at a junior college in San Diego who'd been stealing personnel files during the night shift. It turned out he had sold names, addresses and Social Security numbers to migrant workers who had crossed the border illegally. The story sparked the usual outrage about Mexicans coming into the United States, stealing American jobs, and, now, American identities. But the part of the story that bothered me was that employees were expected to submit personal information that could then be so easily stolen by the likes of a janitor. Or by me and Eddie.

"I just don't want to get in any trouble."

"You won't. Conroy ain't gonna find out."

I thought about it for five seconds less than I should have, and then nodded in agreement.

"We gonna do this?" Eddie clapped his hands together. "Hell yeah. *Hell yeah.*"

Eddie sat low in the driver's seat, his right arm stretched forward to the wheel. He drove the Speedster less enthusiastically than I had expected, but he was playing it cool. Occasionally, he'd look to the back of the car, maybe keeping an eye out for cops. He'd check the oil pressure, watch the odometer, adjust the rear view. He rubbed at the tattoo on his arm.

"How's it healing?" I asked.

"Fine, dude."

"Good," I said. "So how old is your son?"

"He ain't."

"Pardon?"

"He was eight."

"Was?"

Eddie was silent long enough for me to assume the conversation was over. And then he spoke. "He died last year."

"Oh, wow. I'm really sorry. How?"

"Leukemia." He fumbled for a cigarette. I didn't have the heart to tell him he couldn't smoke in the Speedster. The top was down, so Liz wouldn't know. I just hoped he didn't burn a hole in the leather.

"I'm sorry, man," I repeated, uncertain of what else to say. "That sucks."

"It's why I took this gig, man. For the health insurance. Maybe there are more upstanding jobs than this one, but not ones they give an uneducated *spic* like me."

"They have health insurance?" I was contract, not that I would have paid attention. I had health insurance at the newspaper, but I never used it. I signed the forms, I got the card, I threw it in my desk drawer. Eddie gave me a strange look.

"Well," I recovered, "you did what you had to do."

"Tell that to my ex, man. She hates what I do. It made her all jealous and shit. And she's Catholic, you know? She thinks what I do is a sin or something. When my kid died, man, she just split, like it was my fault or something."

"How would it have been your fault?"

"She said it was Jesus punishing me." Eddie laughed and shook his head. "'Cuz I work here."

"Do you believe that?"

"Nah, fuck that." He wiped the tip of his nose with his knuckle. "It's all just superstition, man."

We spoke very little the rest of the trip. Eddie flipped the stereo dial back and forth before settling on a *Tejano* station. He tapped his hands on the wheel in rhythm with the horns.

Eddie parked a block from the office building. He straightened a wrinkle out of his shirt, ran his palm over his stubbly head and rose out of the car, moving briskly toward the building. I spread the tonneau over the car haphazardly and speed-walked after him.

By the time I caught up to Eddie, we had actually turned the corner past Milk-N-It. We walked along the side of the building and into an alley that led us to the company's rust-colored loading dock.

Eddie searched his ring of keys. He unlocked the door, which opened with a loud creak. He nudged me into the dark hallway and quickly closed the door behind us. There was only the light of an exit sign at the end of the hall to guide us as we looked for the stairs. Eddie didn't want to take a chance getting stuck in the elevator after hours.

When we arrived at the fifth floor, Eddie produced another key. He opened the door to the floor and nudged me inside. There was a small door to the right of the assistant's desk marked "private" on a small gold plaque near the top. Eddie produced another key, separate from the others on the ring, and opened the door. He flipped the light switch, and two fluorescent bulbs flickered overhead. The small room looked like it used to be a cleaning closet. The walls were lined with filing cabinets stacked almost to the ceiling. I wasn't sure I could reach the top drawers.

"We need to work fast, dude. *Comprende?*"

"I don't know, Eddie." My palms were sweating. I anxiously wiped them on my jeans. "There's a lot of stuff in here. There must be thousands of files."

"Dude, she's in there somewhere," he said, pointing past my face, "so get to work."

I stumbled to the first filing cabinet, pulled out a drawer and thumbed through the files in earnest. The first folder I searched through contained an autographed glamour shot of a brunette named Stacy. I scanned over her application, which was filled out in blue ballpoint pen with bubbly cursive, circles the size of cupcakes hovering over the *i*s and *j*s. Prior to Milk-N-It, her application stated, Stacy had worked in a strip club in Reno, and before that, as a waitress at Village Inn. There were also photocopies of her medical records, the word "rejected" stamped in red on the top sheet. It was signed illegibly and dated a decade earlier. I slipped the file back into the drawer and moved on to the next.

And the next. And the next. Many of the folders

were stamped "rejected." Some said "dismissed." But I continued to move through each drawer meticulously. Maybe time was a factor, but I worried about skipping over her if I moved too fast. I worried, too, that Eddie would be too quick to write off an entire drawer if he found too many of those "rejected" folders inside, or that he would mistake a younger Indira for somebody else and tuck her folder back into the cabinet.

But I worried too much, I always had, and needlessly so. It took just one more filing cabinet before I found her. Just like that. Easy. Perhaps not as easy as finding her in a magazine under a dumpster, not as easy as folding her into the pocket of my jeans, not as easy as saving her from Kristen. But easy, and uncomplicated. Why hadn't I done this sooner?

"Eddie," I said.

He turned around. "You find it, dude?"

"I found her."

15

I took each step down the stairs triumphantly. I might as well have been skipping. Eddie laughed and shook his head. He knew I was excited.

Indira's folder was tucked tightly under my arm. Eddie had convinced me to take it, swearing that he would bring it back when I was finished with it. He told me no one would miss it; Indira didn't work for Milk-N-It anymore, and hadn't for a while, judging from the materials. In the excitement, I acquiesced. Eddie was putting too much pressure on me in the closet to read the materials anyway.

"Read it when we get outta here, man."

I had just enough time to look at only the second picture of Indira that I had ever seen, a glamour shot, not unlike Stacy's, though it wasn't signed. And I learned her name, Misty. Misty Madsen. "Misty," I whispered, allowing myself a private moment to hear it spoken aloud. "Misty." It was an adjective. It was the name of a frozen drink I got at Dairy Queen when I was a kid. It sounded, same as "Indira," like a porno name.

We hit the last step and galloped to the loading door. I looked through the wire-crossed fire window of the door. Two dark figures emerged out of the dark. I turned to Eddie, worried. He pushed past me and looked out from the corner of the small window.

"Security," he said.

"Security? Eddie!"

"I don't know, holmes. We must have tripped something. I don't know."

We darted back through the hallway and rounded the corner to the lobby door. There was a sign above the handle that warned of an alarm if the door was opened after business hours. Eddie burst through it, and I braced for the shriek of a siren. But the only sound was that of the now recognizable security guards outside. I laughed to myself at the lie that was the sign, at the panic it had induced. Then I took off running into the lobby to catch up.

When I caught up to Eddie, he was standing still in the lobby. I crashed into him, spilling the folder and its contents onto the marbled floor. But I didn't dare pick it up. I didn't want to get anywhere near Conroy.

"Gentleman, so good to see you this evening." Conroy was dressed in a dark suit, a light blue shirt and freshly shined black shoes. He jingled a set of keys in his hand as he pulled the front door closed. "But I must say, I'm disappointed you didn't invite your dear old boss to the party."

Conroy bumped me in the shoulder as he walked past us. I swayed like a Bozo the Clown Bop Bag taking a punch from a five-year-old.

"Look, Mr. Conroy," Eddie said, "I can explain."

"Shush, Eddie," George snapped. Any semblance of amusement on his face was gone. Conroy looked ten years older. He looked more like the czar of porno I had expected at my interview.

"I don't want to hear it," he said, the amused expression returning. Suddenly he was again a picture of congeniality. "You know you're not supposed to be here after hours."

"I was just showing Ethan some pics on the computer," he pleaded, lamely.

Conroy examined the pages on the floor. He looked at Eddie, an eyebrow arched.

"That so?"

"Yeah, man. That down there," Eddie said, pointing, "that's just homework."

"Homework, huh?" Conroy looked over at me, almost for back up, like he couldn't believe this guy would try to pull a fast one on the two of us. "Nice one."

"But chief—"

"You're gone, Eddie."

"C'mon, cuz, I was only—"

"Gone," he repeated.

Eddie stared at Conroy, more stunned than I expected. After all, he claimed to hold his job in disregard.

"Well?" Conroy asked Eddie.

"I need to get my stuff upstairs."

"We'll ship it to you," Conroy said with a wink. "First class."

"Dude over there," Eddie said with a nod directed toward me, "didn't know we weren't supposed to be here. He didn't know, man."

"Goodbye, Eddie," Conroy said like he had just

marked off the last item on his to-do list.

Eddie pursed his lips and moved to the door. I wanted to follow after him, to get out while I could. I had no idea why I was being held back, why Conroy hadn't just fired the both of us at the same time. He walked out and didn't look back. He turned right when he hit pavement, walking slowly in the direction of the Speedster.

"Mr. Ames, won't you do me a favor and pick up this goddamned folder?" Conroy put his hands in his pockets, pushing up the bottom of his suit coat. He looked like he was posing for the cover of *Forbes* or *Esquire*, the young turk, the successful entrepreneur, and only twenty-six! How did he do it? The story inside!

There were always stories like that running in the newspaper. They were all the same. One guy ran a website about tech rumors that sold for $25 million. He was supposedly first on the list to fly privately into space with the Russians. Another started a popular search engine that was later sold to Microsoft. He owned four Lamborghinis. One guy who built custom choppers turned his small company into a hit reality show on the Discovery Channel. He was still reaping the royalties from DVD sales and convention appearances. He didn't work on bikes anymore.

All of those guys, the young turks, the young entrepreneurs, they all got the covers of *Wired, GQ, Newsweek, Time, The New York Times, The Los Angeles Times, The Daily News.*

Conroy was just like them. He was one of them. No doubt.

"Join me upstairs, won't you?" He put a hand on my shoulder and took away the folder. His hand tightened around my arm.

The two security guards came into the lobby. One escorted us to the elevator and the other stayed at the front desk. The elevator doors opened slowly, bouncing along their tracks. George motioned for the guard to stay he where he was.

Conroy whistled "Moon River" in the elevator as it rose to the top floor. He leaned forward to check whether his serenade had gotten my attention or just annoyed me. I remained frozen.

The elevator doors opened. Conroy directed me onto the office floor. He grabbed a pile of mail bound together with a rubber band on top of Lorraine's desk, busily thumbing through the bills and junk mail in his hands. I wished Lorraine was there. She'd clear up the situation with me and Conroy. Over milk and cookies.

"Go into my office," he instructed while sorting his mail. "I'm sure you remember the way."

I walked to the door and tried turning the handle, but it was locked. I looked back at George, who had thrown the mail into a mess on the front desk.

"Oh, don't you have a key?" he asked sarcastically. "Allow me."

He pulled a key from his pocket and jiggled the door open. I walked in and tried not to look for long at any one spot.

Conroy directed me to the same chair I had sat in for my interview. "Sit," he said and walked over to his mini fridge for a bottle of water. There were two framed photos on the shelf behind his desk, where before there had been none. They were photos of Liz. One was of them at a beach. The other was a candid snapshot. He opened his bottle of water and sat at his desk.

"I didn't expect to be back in the goddamned office this evening." Conroy saw me looking at the photographs behind him. He put the water bottle down, grabbed both frames and tossed them into a drawer. "Can't say I was expecting company, either."

"Look, Mr. Conroy, I can explain."

"Jesus Christ, you sound just like your little friend down there." He unbuttoned his suit coat and sat down in his leather chair, leaning back to put his feet up on the desk. "Jesus Christ, you do one favor and then..."

He grabbed the bottle, drank half of the water and spun the cap on the desk.

"Any guesses to where I was going tonight? Where I was heading before I got a call from my friends down there in private security?"

I shook my head.

"I was on my way to a little *din-din* with the proprietor of Voracious. We were going to have martinis," he said, "and a little nosh. Share some goddamned tapas."

Conroy rocked back and forth in his chair.

"And do you know why I was meeting with Voracious?"

I shook my head again.

"Why, they're the biggest name in adult entertainment. Or don't you know?"

"You had mentioned that, yes."

"Well, we're merging with Voracious, Ethan. It's the way this business is going. They're like the Super Wal-Mart of porn. They're eating up all the goddamned competitors like us, the ones fighting the good fight."

He folded his hands on the desk and leaned forward.

"They've got us beat, though, hands down. And you know what? Doesn't matter, not one goddamned bit. Because Milk-N-It is about to become one of the biggest names in adult entertainment."

He slammed the last of the water and chucked the bottle into a garbage can underneath his desk.

"Guess I won't be *leasing* Porsches anymore."

"Lucky you," I said.

"Right. Lucky me. But let's talk about unlucky you. Right now I should be closing this deal right now over a bowl of *ceviche* instead of sitting in my office after hours because two ex-employees decided to raid the castle."

Ex-employees. It was not subtle.

"What were you doing here tonight?"

"I was looking for someone."

"I can see that." He grabbed the folder off the desk and flipped through it. "*Tight Horizons*. Now there's one we'd all like to forget," he said smugly. "Tell me, Mr. Ames, what's your interest in Indira?"

"Misty."

"Of course. *Misty*," he said, looking over her information in the folder. "I forgot you're on such good terms. So what's your angle?"

"No angle. I just wanted to meet her."

"See," he said, throwing his hands up in the air, "that's what's wrong with this business. This ain't Hollywood, kid. She ain't no Marilyn Monroe."

"What's that supposed to mean?"

"You want to meet a girl in one of my magazines."

"So?"

"You love her?"

"Come on." I knew he was messing with me.

"Do ya?"

"I don't know."

"Of course you do. Jesus Christ."

"Maybe."

"Jesus Christ. Don't any of you freaks just want to get off anymore?"

"It's not like that."

"It's not, huh? Listen, guy, you can't love these bitches. They're goddamned nut jobs, guy. Filthy, unlovable, crack whores. You don't want anything to do with these girls. Believe me."

"Maybe that's because of the way you treat them," I choked out.

He just laughed. "Noble, guy. Very noble."

"Whatever."

"You know, it's not really your fault. I blame it on Voracious. They started all this goddamned nonsense," he said, almost exasperated. "You think you're the only one? Listen, guy, we hear from freaks like you all the time. They call, they e-mail, they get all nerdy at the conventions, latched on to Mary Manner like a monkey on a tree. It's all become so *personal*. This business should have stayed in the seedy theater where it belonged."

"Why is that?"

"Because there was no tape to rewind over and over and over again. It was tits, pussy, orgasm," he said, slicing each word in the air with his hand, "and that was it."

"That's it, huh?"

"There was no staring at a chick's face over and over again, as if she somehow actually *gave* you the orgasm. She didn't! It's just you, sitting there with your dick in your hand, hunkered over a million pixels of light with your pants down. She didn't jerk your chain. You did, guy."

He put his arms behind his head and leaned back in his chair. "But, anyway, that's business. And speaking of business," he said, "you're fired."

I stood up, took note of the pictures of Liz that Conroy had apparently hidden during our last encounter.

"I'll say hello to Liz for you."

"You do that," he taunted.

Then I eyeballed the folder on the desk.

"Now, now, I'll be keeping this," he said with a knowing smile. "And this goes for both you and your pal Eddie: If I find anything out of order here, I'm coming after you. And you won't like it when I find you."

16

When I pulled up to Liz's place, I heard thumping reggae and people talking at the top of their voices from somewhere nearby. I wondered if the noise was keeping her awake. I hoped so. It was late, but I wanted to talk.

I killed the engine and rose slowly out of the car, my limbs numb from the long ride, the rumble of the old racing engine and the work of shifting and steering manually. The collar of my shirt was loosened, and my tie was no longer wrapped around my neck, but draped over my shoulders like a scarf. I'd spent the evening in a summery sweat, a result of the day's events and time spent in a sports car with the top down and no air conditioning. My undershirt felt like it had been pulled from the bottom of a gym locker. It probably smelled that way, too.

I looked toward the ocean and savored its proximity. The air drifting in from the beach was cool and salty and wet.

The music and the chatter grew louder as I walked up the stairs, stoking a headache that had been brewing since I'd left Conroy's office. All I wanted was to shower, to eat a little and to find out why Liz was dating a guy like George Conroy, and why she hadn't told me. But that wouldn't be happening. The music, the party, it was coming from Liz's.

Clark spotted me first. He flicked his fingers daintily in the air, like a southern belle spotting her horse at the Kentucky Derby. It was easy to see that he was hammered. Some of the guys from the sports desk were huddled around him, as well as the photo editor, a quiet guy named Sam who I'd rarely seen engage in a conversation with anyone. But he was in near hysterics. They all were. Clark had probably just told another one of his sex jokes. It was like candy for those guys.

But the way they were huddled together, they looked like street urchins scheming to pickpocket the rich guy before he hopped into his Rolls. I wondered if it wasn't a sex joke they were laughing at but something else. Something like the contents of my bag? They did, after all, keep looking in my direction, like the joke was on me. And I wouldn't have put it past Clark or one of the sports guys to rummage through my stuff.

I moved toward the group, but a girl bumped into me with her plastic cup, spilling foam on my coat.

"Your suit," she said, wiping the suds off the pocket flap. "I'm so sorry."

She was not unattractive, though she did her best to appear otherwise. She had extremely short bangs and her shoulder-length hair was dyed an unnatural red. There was a small, silver hoop through one nostril, which was cute, and an eyebrow ring with a silver ball on each end, which was not.

"That's OK," I said. "It needed dry cleaned anyway."

"Then I'm glad I could be of help."

There was still a little beer left in her cup, which she quickly tipped to her mouth and swallowed. When she lowered her cup, she was smiling. There was foam on her lip.

"So," she said, "you work at the paper? You look kinda familiar."

"Yeah," I replied, looking beyond her toward Clark. "I thought the same thing."

She was the education reporter at the Vista bureau, she said, and raised a hand to introduce herself. That glob of foam was still on her face.

"Excuse me for a second," I said. She raised her eyebrows and nodded, taking a drink from her cup.

I walked the perimeter of the living room. Stacks of CDs from the morning were arranged neatly on the shelves above the stereo. Liz's signature pile of newspapers and coffee cups were gone from the ottoman. Her unfinished paintings were neatly stacked against a wall in the dining room. Maybe she'd stored my bag somewhere safe.

Heading back toward the bedroom, I parted the crowd, walking by my new friend with the piercings.

"Guys nowadays," I heard her saying to another girl I didn't recognize.

"So fucking aloof," the girl said, nodding her head to the beat.

I found Liz in the kitchen blending ice with a blue liquid, martini glasses with cactus-shaped stems splayed in front of her. When she saw me, Liz turned off the blender. It ground to a halt, and chunks of ice floated to the top like bloated bodies from a sunken ship. The crowd gathered behind her moaned in disappointment.

"Ethan!" She threw her arms around me. Her breath smelled strongly of tequila.

This was the happiest Liz had been since I'd taken up residence on her couch. She enjoyed the congestion of people, of the music, of the spilled liquor on the Persian rugs. But I found it irritating. She could tell. She squeezed my arms with her hands, looking into my eyes like a father sizing up his prodigal son. I couldn't tell whether it was a warm embrace or if she was using me to steady herself.

"What's wrong?"

Before I could fill her in, though, I spotted Jasper, clad in his short shorts and a loose Hawaiian shirt with a classic-car pattern. He was trying to mingle with Clark and the others. He had no idea that the very group he was trying to penetrate was the same group that mocked the smarmy tone he took in his verbose columns about Soroptimist pancake breakfasts and cancer-stricken Girl Scouts. I almost felt bad for him, until I noticed he was holding two cups. Until I saw him hand one to Kristen.

Jasper saw that I was watching them. He raised his cup and smiled. I did not return the toast.

"Maybe we should talk about this after the party," I told Liz. "Why is Kristen here? How did she get here? Did she come with... Jasper?"

"Don't worry, Ethan. It's OK." Liz squeezed my hand, her speech slurred. "I invited them because it's OK."

"Really? She really is?" I snapped. "Did you know

that? Did you know that and invite them anyway?"

"Yes," she replied, her eyebrows suddenly furled. The way Liz pouted, she resembled Audrey Hepburn. "It's my house."

"Never mind," I said, plotting my retreat. I still had the car keys, after all. "You're right. It's your house."

"Thank you," she said. "So, are you OK?"

"Not really. But it's been a shitty enough day already, so why stop now?"

"What do you mean? What happened?"

"Put it this way," I replied as discreetly as I could when surrounded by a bunch of reporters. "I'm out a job."

"What?" Liz asked angrily. She seemed genuinely surprised, but I assumed she already knew. I figured Conroy would have at least called her. I tried to hush her, she was talking so loudly, but Liz was undeterred.

"He fired you?" The volume at which she spoke made the word *fired* rise above the noisy chatter as though an exclamation point had become stuck on a computer keyboard, shooting rapid-fire punctuation across the page.

"Liz, please."

"What happened?" she whispered with a giggle, like we were playing "Hide and Seek" and she was hidden in plain sight.

"Well, after work, Eddie and I went to the office."

"After hours?"

"Yeah."

"Uh oh."

"Uh oh, what?"

"Nothing. So then what?"

"We started digging through the Human Resources

files there."

"Oh, Ethan."

"Yeah, well, I found Indira's file. Her name is Misty."

"You did! That's great news."

"It was, until Conroy showed up. He fired Eddie, just booted him out of the building. Then, only after he tortured me in his office—"

"*Tortured?*" she asked, half concerned, half sarcastic. She sipped from her drink.

"Yes. Mentally tortured. Anyway, then he fired me, too."

"Shit. Ethan?" Liz put her hand over her mouth. "*Shit.*"

"Yeah, what a dick." I waited for a reaction, but she ignored it.

"Liz," I tried again, "I saw some things in there, in Conroy's office."

She raised an eyebrow. "What things?"

"Well—"

"Yes, Ethan, what did you see?"

I turned around.

There was Kristen, her arms folded tautly across her chest. I had no idea how long she'd been standing there, but I had a feeling it had been a while.

17

"I'm glad you came," Liz told her, a gesture intended to diffuse the tension. But if I was shocked to see Kristen with Jasper, then she was probably thinking the same thing about me and Liz. "Are you having a good time?"

"Yeah. It's just great," she replied disingenuously. I stared at my shoes.

"Oh, good." Liz tapped the side of her empty cup with her fingernails and drunkenly swayed side to side. I wanted to reach out and steady her, but I had to steady myself first.

The thirsty group still standing around the blender chanted for Liz like they were cheering on a football team, and she found her excuse to leave.

"I better get in there before they riot."

Liz squeezed my arm warmly and moved to the kitchen. I tried not to follow her with my eyes.

"I guess they've never used a blender before," I joked.

Kristen didn't laugh.

"So where were you?" she asked, observing my wrinkled suit. "You don't work nights anymore." She paused. "Or do you?"

"Well—"

"Never mind. It's not my business anymore."

She was right, though I had the urge to tell her anyway. It had been my habit to tell Kristen everything. Well, almost everything.

"Nowhere."

"Oh."

"Yeah. So."

"So."

"Can I have my security deposit back?" I asked. We had no trouble picking up where we had left off. We never had.

"Should I send it to this address?"

"No, I can come by Jasper's later. Just leave it under a flower pot, OK?"

No trouble at all. We were like negative ends of magnets being forced together. Avoiding eye contact at all costs, we craned our necks away from each other, like we were watching two parades pass by on opposing streets.

"This is ridiculous," she announced. "Let's just go outside."

There was a story in the travel section of the newspaper about seeing Europe on the cheap. The story went into great detail about all of the places to visit that were free or only required a nominal fee. There were sidebars on youth hostels, on finding the right Eurail pass, on the best bakeries. A break-out box suggested buying blocks of cheese, fresh bread and a bottle of pilsner from a small market for a frugal European lunch.

Kristen was immediately smitten with the idea of just such a trip, and of course it was one that I'd wanted to take since meeting Tabitha. We went during our last spring break before graduation. Kristen's dad gave her the airplane ticket as an early graduation present, and he even gave me thousands of airline miles so I could afford my own. I envisioned a week of guzzling hefeweizen in the streets of Munich, eating our way through the best Parisian restaurants and partying all night at an Italian disco, all the while secretly seeing the sites Tabitha had described to me while we cuddled on the couch. But Kristen had something entirely different in mind. The trip should be an educational experience, she lectured. And she made certain that it was. While she forged through every major museum on the continent, carrying only a small purse and a pocket map, I trailed her with our heavy suitcases, which rattled and bounced over every bump of the continent's cobblestone streets.

I stopped on a corner, exhausted and disgusted by her behavior. I regretted taking the free miles from her father, and on that corner, I plotted how I could repay him before I left Kristen. I had plenty of time to consider it. She had gone a block before she noticed that I had lagged behind. Annoyed, she insisted that I keep up.

"You're drawing attention to us," she snapped at me. "We don't want to look like tourists."

As Kristen waded through the crowd gathered near Liz's front door, she looked back at me with the same impatience she had shown in Europe. I thought again about how miserable I had been on that trip, and how I had planned to end it when we got home. So why had I followed Kristen to California, and why was I now following her out the door?

As we cleared the crowd, Liz watched us from the kitchen like a lighthouse spotting a fishing boat lost in the fog. After I stepped outside, Kristen closed the door behind us with a huff.

Kristen leaned against the railing across from the landing and sipped from a plastic cup. She looked over my shoulder to the house.

"Expecting someone?" I asked.

"Wouldn't you like to know?"

"Not really."

"Typical."

"What was that?"

"Never mind. So how's the magazine business, Ethan? Picked up any good pictures lately?" She patted my front pockets with her palms, daring me into a fight. "Sorry the last one got all ripped up. An honest mistake."

I brushed her hand away. Tiny spit bubbles formed in the corner of her mouth, remnants of a speech impediment from her youth. Kristen had been drinking heavily—and likely on an empty stomach.

"Do you know how embarrassing this has been?" she continued. "I mean, the pornography, that was between you and me. But then you quit the paper? What does that even look like?"

I didn't know what she was so embarrassed about. It wasn't like she had to explain at work. Her contact with people from the paper was limited to occasionally bumping into one of the cub reporters on the complex. At the PR firm, she could tell them whatever she thought they'd believe. That's what you do at those places.

"I know you're embarrassed about all of this, Kristen, but I would think you'd be more worried about how it looks dating a forty-five-year-old dude with a cat and a Camaro."

"You don't get to judge me."

"No, I'm well aware of that."

"You just don't get it, Ethan. You never did. You think it's somehow the same thing. But it isn't. What do people think of someone whose boyfriend wants to fuck a porn star, so much so, in fact, that he goes to work at a porn magazine?"

"They do video now, actually."

She recoiled. "I don't care what they do."

"And didn't you mean ex-boyfriend?"

"Yes, I did. *Ex*-boyfriend."

"Just so it's official," I said. "I wasn't exactly sure."

"Oh, so you didn't know that we were through?" she asked sarcastically. "That's why you left the key in an envelope under my door?"

"Well, we've done this so many times before."

"Let me clear it up for you, Ethan," she said. "We're done. And yes, I'm with Jasper."

"Right, Jasper. How'd you end up with a guy like that?"

"Just lucky, I guess."

"The topless car washing? The Frisbee playing?"

"Yes?"

"All those times we made fun of the guy, what, were you just waiting to hook up with him?"

"Yes, Ethan, I was just 'waiting to hook up.' What can I say? I needed someone who carried a wallet in his pocket, not pornography."

"Look, I didn't think you'd find that," I said.

"And that's supposed to make it all OK?"

"No. I'm just saying that I didn't mean for it to happen. It was stupid." But it wasn't stupid. It was Indira. If it was a careless move, it didn't matter. I had been careless for a reason. I think I knew it then. I definitely knew it now.

"Look, Kristen, it's been a long night. I'm not sure what we're doing out here. What is it you want?"

"An apology, for starters."

"Well, I just apologized, and you didn't accept."

"Give me a break. There are consequences for your actions, you know." Her eyes welled. She was always an emotional drinker.

"I understand there are consequences. I seem to recall getting kicked out of my own apartment."

"You kicked yourself out." She poked her finger into my chest repeatedly like she was playing Pin the Tail on the Donkey. I grabbed her hand and squeezed, pushing her pointed finger into her clasped hand with my thumb.

"Don't," I warned, "touch me."

Kristen twisted her hand in mine. I felt her fingers contract and her knuckles shift as she tried to free herself, like a magician slipping out of a straightjacket. I held tight. In a way, it felt like a game, a leisurely one I was winning.

"Let go," she said indignantly. Her free hand balled into a fist, and I steeled myself. And yet, whatever was about to happen, I wasn't going to let go.

But she didn't hit me. Instead, she glanced over my shoulder, and her fingers went limp in my hand. Her clenched fist fell open. I turned around to see what had diffused the ticking time bomb. It was Jasper, watching from the window. I let go of her hand and waved him away, but he ignored me. His focus was on her.

She smiled and nodded several times, as if they had just communicated an inside joke. She wiped her eyes and, after nodding again, watched him move away from the window.

I wanted to believe that all Jasper was doing in the window was posturing. He didn't strike me as the type who had ever been in a fight or come to the rescue of anyone, no matter how noble the notion. But if Kristen had signaled differently, if it had been necessary, he would have fought for her, and I knew it. It wasn't caution or hesitation that Jasper had exercised. It was prudence.

There were times when I looked at Indira and felt such anger toward the men who had used her or taken advantage of her. Men who fucked her on cue, just like those who gangbanged my tour guide at the Milk-N-It shoot. Men like George Conroy, who made his buck off Indira and then put her through the paper shredder. I had always thought of Indira as a helpless beauty, a victim of circumstance, an unwitting participant in a vile, defeating line of work. Out there with Kristen, it was like a blindfold had been lifted from over my eyes, if only for a moment, and I knew what I saw in Indira's printed gaze wasn't helplessness. It was resignation. I saw it my tour guide when she rested on the towel. I saw it, too, in Kristen as we stood on the landing, and I watched it melt away when Jasper appeared at the window.

"Well," she said, "I can see this is going nowhere." Kristen wiped her eyes with a rumpled tissue produced from her pocket.

My throat was dry. I no longer wished for a beer but now for water. It was several hours since I'd had any.

"For what it's worth," I said, unexpectedly, my heart pounding in my ears, "I'm sorry."

"You're sorry?" she repeated, suspiciously. "What are you sorry for?"

I glanced back at the house and wiped the pasty corners of my lips. "I'm sorry, just about everything. Really."

Kristen studied my face and then shrugged. Did I look anything like she did when I stared at Indira?

"It's fine." She practically swallowed the words. "Good luck, I guess, with the whole magazine, um, with that whole thing."

And just like that, she returned to the party.

I leaned over the railing and looked down the row of parking spots to Liz's car. I reached into my pocket and cradled the keys in my fingers. Maybe I would drive down to the corner for a bottle of water. Maybe I would just keep on driving after that.

Liz came outside, beer in hand. I dropped the keys back into my pocket.

"Hey, kid. You look like you could use this."

"Definitely." I took several gulps. It wasn't water, but it was wet.

"Everything go OK?" she asked.

"I suppose." I rubbed my eyes. "There were just some things that needed to be said. Been a weird night, though."

Liz grabbed my cup and put it on the railing next to hers. She wrapped her tiny, golden arms around my waist and leaned into my chest. I rested my chin on her head and peered through the curtains into her house. Inside, I could see only the faceless outlines of people, hoisting cups, bumping into one another, spilling beer, whooping, hooting, jumping, laughing, dancing and yelling. Nobody stopped to peer out past the curtains back at us.

Liz held on for a long time, to the point where I thought she had passed out, because she barely moved, and she uttered not a word. She just breathed deep and steady, in rhythm with the beat of bossa nova coming from inside. Only when someone had the stereo and sent the stylus scratching along the grooves of the record did Liz finally stir.

"Nice party." I nodded toward the door. "Your record collection might not survive it though."

"Oh, God." She looked up, sleepily.

"Didn't you know you should never, ever give journalists free booze?"

"So I've heard. I better go lock up the liquor cabinet before they tear the place apart."

"Good idea. Liz?"

"Yeah?"

"My bag?"

"It's safe," she assured me. "It's under my bed."

She grabbed my hand.

"Come on, Ames," she said. "Let's go save my record shelves."

18

Bottles accumulated in the recycling bin next to the fridge throughout the night, piled like bodies flung into a mass grave. Wine glasses, corks and half-empty bowls of wilted citrus wedges lined the kitchen counter and dining table. A sobered Liz worked to push the last of the drunks out the door.

Jasper and Kristen had left a few hours before. I had waved goodbye to Kristen while Jasper helped her with her jacket, but she didn't wave back. Either she hadn't seen me or she pretended not to.

Clark threw his spent bottle on top of the others. Several toppled onto the floor. The sound at that hour was as jarring as an alarm clock.

"Oops," he said, and then grabbed two fresh bottles out of the fridge. He popped the tops and swallowed a mouthful of beer before he handed me the other bottle. Then he swallowed some more.

"Come, Ethan, talk to me of world affairs." Clark threw his arm over my shoulder and guided me to the couch, the bottle in his hand slung over my chest. It was nearly empty.

"I'm a little behind on the news these days."

"Right," he said, belching discreetly, "because of the porn business? How's that going? Banging lots of chicks?"

"You know me."

"He's not getting any!" Clark announced, as if he had an audience of someone other than me.

When Liz had managed to get the last person out the door, she began to clean up, sifting through the debris on the floor. She carried a load into the kitchen. Glass clanked and the faucet ran. When Liz returned, she was sipping from a glass of water and carrying a box of wooden matches. She moved throughout the house lighting candles scented with sandalwood and lavender. The smell was smoky and sweet. The dull glow felt holy.

"Miss Carlisle, you throw one *helluva* party," Clark declared, swinging the neck of the empty bottle between two fingers.

"Thanks." Liz went back to the kitchen for his refill. She placed it on the floor next to the Gatsby chair and tapped his knee. "Now move."

Like a dog following a treat, Clark relocated without complaint. He hoisted the fresh bottle to his mouth.

"Careful," Liz warned affectionately as she wrapped her legs in a fleece blanket. "You might just get drunk."

"With any luck," he replied. "So, Ethan, what was the fracas out there with your old girl?"

"Fracas" was an inside joke. Back on the desk, Clark encouraged the young copy editors to pepper their headlines with odd, dated or challenging words—anything to "get the reader thinking," he said. All it really did was get us into trouble. The idea was to keep headlines at the fourth-grade reading level, not to play a game of Scrabble. It pleased Clark to no end—not because we did the wrong thing but because he persuaded us to do it. Clark once convinced me to describe a trio of local businessmen who were seizing foreclosed homes as a "troika." The next day, a tear sheet was on my desk, the headline circled with a red Sharpie and a sticky note next to it from the editor. "See me," it said. When we complained to Clark that he was getting us into trouble, he shrugged off the idea. "Call it a character-building exercise," he said.

"Ethan owed Kristen an apology," Liz said.

Clark chuckled knowingly. "What, for going off to work in adult entertainment? Hey, who hasn't been *there*?"

"It wasn't like that," I said.

"No? Well, that's the rumor. And you know what we do with rumors in this business."

"I become more cynical every day."

"I hear you. Still, smart move."

"Quitting the newspaper? Sometimes I think so," I said, though at the moment I didn't think it was such a good idea. And then I realized what Clark meant. "Oh, you mean the porno thing."

"Quite the contrary." He leaned forward, put his elbows on his knees and folded his hands. "Apologizing. It was smart. It was good."

"You think so?"

"I know so."

He stared at me, though it was not his custom—

Clark rarely made eye contact. He massaged the sides of his face. The sleeves of his plaid shirt hung from his bones like a weathered tarp slipping through the attic rafters. His hands were wrinkled and leathery, the hands of a Montana rancher, not a lifelong newspaperman. I always thought it was compulsive smoking that made Clark appear ten years older than he really was. But maybe that wasn't it at all. They weren't the wrinkles of Keith Richards. They were Brian Wilson's.

"What's up, Clark?" Liz asked.

"Nothing."

"Go ahead if you've got something to say."

"I don't." He took a swig. "It doesn't matter."

"Yes, it does," she prodded gently. It was how I imagined Liz conducted herself during the most sensitive of interviews.

"It's nothing," he said. "It's not like I went to work for a girlie magazine or anything."

"Come on, Clark," I said in the same peer-pressuring manner that he had invoked on the copy editors. "Spill the beans."

"OK, OK, I'll *spill the beans,*" he said, mocking me on his way to the fridge. Clark hadn't finished the bottle Liz had brought him, and yet he was off to retrieve another. When he returned, he asked Liz if he could smoke in the house.

"No, you may not."

He put away his pack.

"So?" she asked.

"It was a long time ago."

"What was a long time ago?"

"Well, there was this girl. Are you sure I can't smoke in here?"

"I'm sure. You were saying?"

"There was this girl. And it's very possible, well, I've always figured, at least, that things might have gone too far."

"What do you mean, 'gone too far'?" Liz asked. "You don't mean—"

"Not really. Not in the classic sense, anyway. I didn't hold her down or anything. But I knew she didn't want to. I kind of pushed her into it. Manipulated her."

There was a story in the newspaper about a group of flower children-turned-activists who had robbed a bank in the Seventies, the culmination of several violent protests against the Vietnam War. (The group later admitted that the stolen money would have been used to travel overseas to protest the violence.) During the heist, a guard at the bank was shot and killed. Though at the time, most of the group were arrested, two members escaped. For thirty years they eluded the authorities. Then one was discovered, working, ironically, as a bank teller in Montana. According to the story, prosecutors offered her a deal: lessened jail time if she revealed the location of that last group member. She refused. They put her away for life.

As we worked on the headline for that story, Clark commented that the group had the best of intentions in mind, that the war was indeed bullshit.

"You're joking, right?" I asked.

"They did a lot of good," he said.

I half-kidded myself at the time that Clark was that last group member. But there were plenty of moments after when I didn't think it was so far-fetched.

I would never have thought Clark was the kind of

guy who had led a perfect life. He didn't, however, strike me as someone who carried with him a guilty conscience—Clark was about as emotional as a water buffalo. And yet, revealing this secret clearly pained him. Had Clark admitted to being that last group member, he might have done it bragging, guns blazing. Instead, he seemed near tears.

"She was your girlfriend?" Liz asked carefully.

"Not really. We weren't dating or anything. She was just a girl from my neighborhood. I don't know if she'd ever even had a boyfriend before. She was only four-teen, you know? Her breath still smelled sweet, like when you're a kid and all you eat is candy."

"What happened?"

"I got her to throw a house party while her parents were away. Quite the rager. Kind of like this little soirée." He tapped Liz on the shoulder admiringly.

"They had a pool in the back yard. This was unheard of in Montana. I think they kept it filled maybe three months out of the year, otherwise the thing would have turned into an ice rink. My buddies and me used to sneak into it sometimes in the middle of the night, even before I met her. All the kids did. Her parents must have been oblivious. Or I don't know. Maybe they weren't. Maybe they just didn't care. They were really unhappy people. I heard they slept in separate rooms.

"Anyway, later that night at the party, some of us went for a skinny dip." He chuckled, but it was a dark, guttural release. "Good thing the water was heavily chlorinated."

"Jesus, Clark," I said.

Liz shook her head at me. "Go ahead, Clark."

"I think it must have been enormous pressure to be

with an older guy, with all those older people around. If she said no, she wasn't just rejecting sex. I guess she was rejecting social advancement."

"You're over-thinking it," Liz assured him.

"Yeah, I know. I was eighteen. All I wanted was pussy. Obviously I didn't think about it in those terms. But I'm not sure how that makes it OK." He looked to Liz. "It's not OK, right?"

I was about to offer my opinion, but she chimed in first.

"Listen, girls are used to that kind of pressure. Girls know how to say no."

"At fourteen?"

"At fourteen."

"What bothers me about it most is I didn't even want her that bad. I knew it going into it. But she kept coming back for more. She'd call, but I'd never answer. She'd knock on my door, but I'd never answer. I let my folks get it. They thought she was some junior high kid selling cookies for a fundraiser or something."

"Stockholm Syndrome," I said. Liz glared.

"Yeah," he said, laughing uncomfortably, "maybe so. Anyway, she became quite a nympho after that. Really fucked around. Slept with dudes way older than me."

"Poor Clark," Liz said. "Don't beat yourself up".

"Well, you know, I can't help but feel a *little* responsible. Don't you think?"

"Why? Because she went on to enjoy it? It was her decision."

Clark seemed startled by her reaction. I was, too.

"I'm not so sure it was."

"Even if it wasn't, what can you do about it now? Nothing. Listen, Clark, I'm sure she's fine."

I wondered how Liz could so cavalier. It was a betrayal to all the women she had interviewed, so battered and bruised by sex. The stories Liz had written, the pieces that had won her awards and clout, they might as well have been plagiarized. Liz wasn't in their corner. She never had been.

"Maybe not," I interjected. "I think you could still do something about it, Clark. You could find her."

Liz raised an eyebrow.

"I've been married twenty-five years, dude. I have two teenagers." It was the first time Clark alluded to the concerns of his family since I'd known him. It was a reminder that he was out late, getting drunk with people half his age. He wasn't at home with them, where he belonged.

"You're right, Liz. It's been so long, I probably don't even have the story straight. How about some tunes, Ethan?" he asked, and then turned to Liz. "Got any Zeppelin?"

She directed me to a row of albums along the top shelf. I grabbed the first Zeppelin I found and put it on the turntable. Clark emptied the second bottle with a big swig and started in on the next. He rested his head against the back of the chair. "Skip ahead to 'The Rain Song.' I like that one."

We listened without a word. I stewed silently, wincing whenever Liz reached to tickle my fingertips or remove a piece of fuzz from my suit pants. When the side ended, I asked Clark what he wanted to hear next.

"Just flip it," she said, nodding toward Clark. He was slumped to the side of the armchair, out cold.

"He'll probably regret all that tomorrow," I said like

it was her fault.

Liz seemed puzzled by my tenor. "We'll see."

She covered him with her fleece blanket and returned to the couch, dipping her toes under my leg like she was testing the temperature of a bath.

"Sorry about the party. I know you didn't expect to come home to that," she said. "But I hadn't heard from you, and then it started to get late. I didn't even know if you'd be coming home at all."

"What did you think happened?"

"I don't know. I thought maybe you'd found her, or maybe got a good lead on her or something."

"Don't you think I would have called you?"

"I don't know."

"You could have called."

"I didn't want to interrupt, I guess."

"Interrupt?"

"Anyway, so what did George say to you?"

"Liz, how well do you know that guy?"

"What do you mean?"

"I thought George Conroy was just some guy in the industry you'd come across on your beat."

"Yes. And?"

"And... Well, I saw some things in his office."

"What things?" She was cool and suspicious.

"Pictures of you. One was with him."

"Oh." She said it as though she had been caught hiding birthday presents from a child.

"Please tell me he's your stepbrother or a former co-worker. Your gay best friend."

"I can't do that."

"Are you *dating* that prick?"

She shifted to the opposite end of the couch. "That's

a nice thing to say."

"Liz?"

She hesitated. "Yes. Well, sort of."

I threw my arms into the air.

"Calm down," she disciplined. "It's not a big deal."

"Not a big deal?" I yelled, my face reddening. I didn't care if Clark woke up, unlikely though it was. "How can you date a guy like that?"

"'Dating' is probably strong. It's been on and off since college. It's a convenience thing, really. I'm not sure how convenient it is anymore." The last part she said to herself.

"Convenient? You do understand what he does for a living?"

"Yes. So do you. But I guess that wasn't such a problem when he might have been of use to you."

"There's a big difference between what I did and what you are doing. I assume you're sleeping with the guy. Right?

"I have, yes."

"Have you since we, you know?"

"That's what you're worried about?" she snapped.

Given Conroy's line of work, I assumed he got around, and I was suddenly consumed with a fear of contracting an STD. It was a paranoia I hadn't experienced since my first naive encounters with sex in college. And yet, I wouldn't have thought twice about it with Indira.

"It doesn't worry you? Maybe I don't know you as well as I thought."

"And why is that?" Liz had kept her cool, but she was starting to simmer.

"First you tell Clark all that crap, that it was OK to

push that girl into sex, and then you admit to being involved—secretly, I might add—with a guy like Conroy."

"I thought you might be sympathetic."

"He uses people, Liz. In the worst way."

"But not you, right?" She scrunched a pillow under her arms. "Tell me something. What if you'd found Indira's address tonight? What if she'd fucked your brains out? What would you have done?"

"I highly doubt that would have happened."

"I bet you would have rushed over here to tell me all about it and then still tried to get me on the couch. You get mad at Clark, you get mad at me for dismissing his past transgressions, but you would have done the same thing. You're a user. Everyone is. So don't start acting all goddamned virtuous."

"Wow. You even sound like him."

"At least I know who I sound like." Her voice cracked.

"What's that supposed to mean?"

"You don't get it. You're like Clark's girlfriend, too stupid to understand that nobody's gonna answer the door when she knocks."

Liz tossed the pillow against my leg and rose from the couch. She adjusted the wrinkles in her jeans and brushed the front of them as though she'd just been in a back-alley brawl.

"I'm going to bed. Let me know when he's awake," she said curtly, pointing to Clark. "I'll call a cab."

"Was this was all just a joke, then?" I asked after her, caring very little about how Clark got home. "I mean, why keep me around if you had Conroy this whole time?"

"Wouldn't you want more?" she said, standing in the doorway of her bedroom. "Shouldn't I?" And then she closed the door behind her.

I thought about what she had said. I knew she wasn't just talking about Conroy. She was talking about Kristen and she was talking about herself. I realized then how cruel it was to have used them. It was cruel because they knew they'd been used.

Sleeping on Liz's couch, driving Liz's car, lying in Liz's bed, I often wondered what I had done to deserve her comfort and care. I had always felt like I had cheated, like I was enjoying the spoils of someone else's war. Liz was only thirty, and already she had so much, her career, her house on the beach, her car. Why wouldn't she have a guy like Conroy waiting in the wings, someone with money and power and a car to beat her own? Those were the things I presumed she needed, the things I didn't have. After all, I was just a scrawny, confused kid who would never turn the page on Tabitha, on *Record Shelves*, on Indira, the guy who would always be one step behind his dreams.

But that was just it. That was the allure, the reason Liz had used *me*. Because she had. Liz had used me because I was everything she was not.

19

Clark cleared his throat, and the rumble of smoker's phlegm in the otherwise quiet house awoke me. I lay still, watching him tap his fist to his chest repeatedly like a bongo. The music he made was the product of acid reflux. I recognized the sound from my father's own noisy, sleepless nights.

I rested my head against the arm of the love seat, and rescued a half-full beer bottle between my legs before it tipped over. Clark turned on the lamp on the end table near my feet.

I yawned, and even the smallest movement made my head spin. If I was still drunk, surely Clark was, too. "Want a cab?"

He massaged the back of his neck as though he was considering my offer. Then he reached for his coat, just like I knew he would. "Thanks, but no thanks. I got a few years on you, dude. I know what I'm doing."

I nodded slowly and blinked.

"I better get going."

"OK."

"It's late."

"Right."

"You know, I was thinking, Ethan, if I could, I might try to do something," he said. "I'd probably try to find her or something, like you said, if there weren't so many variables to consider."

"But I won't let it control the rest of my life." He waited for a comment. I picked my eye.

"Anyway, drop an e-mail every once in a while, alright? Let me know if you see any pierced clits." Clark opened the door. His slinking framed moved to the stairs, and his head bobbed as he walked to the parking lot below.

I looked back at Liz's bedroom, hoping that Clark's exit had roused her. I wanted to put my ear close to her door and listen to hear if she had been stirred. But I didn't. I looked up at the ceiling and imagined where I would go in the morning. My time with Liz had come to an end. I didn't need to be told. I drifted back to sleep and had angry, turbulent dreams.

In the morning, the curtains were drawn, and bright, radiant light filled the house. I was tangled in the blanket Liz had first draped over Clark. Disoriented, I sat up slowly and held my aching head. I put my feet on the floor to ease the spinning, and a yellow sticky note fell to the ground. I bent down to grab it and called out to Liz. Her bedroom door was open, but she didn't answer.

I read the note: "1220 P Street, Apt. 203, Sacramento. Car keys are on the table."

I grabbed my cell phone and sent Liz a text. "This what I think it is? Where did you get it?"

My phone buzzed almost immediately. "Where do you think?"

"Thanks," I keyed back, hoping Liz would accept it as gratitude and an apology. But she didn't reply.

I held tight to the slip of paper, refusing to part with it, to risk Kristen tearing it to shreds or Conroy locking it in a drawer. I carried the note into the bathroom and memorized the address as I urinated. I put on my jeans and secured the note in my pocket. And as I finished dressing, I practiced the first words I'd say to Misty Madsen. They had to be the right words. Exactly right.

20

The green, sprawling farmland along the interstate was soaked with rain. Water dripped through the cracks of the Speedster's soft top and clouded the windshield. I turned on the rickety heater, which slowly cleared the condensation off the glass. I pulled the sleeve of my fleece over my hand and rubbed it like a squeegee across the windshield, wiping away the frame of moisture that remained.

Drivers were moving nervously in the rain, stopping and starting erratically. The taillights of the cars ahead flashed and blinked like Christmas trees. I was exhausted, nursing a hangover, and their glow easily lulled me into a dangerous trance.

When I got to Sacramento, it was dark and I was ready for sleep. I took a room in the first motel I found. Inside, I put my bags in the closet and fell on the bed. I propped my head on two old pillows whose cushioning had long since given out. I grabbed the TV remote on the nightstand and flipped through twenty-

two channels of nothing special. I watched the clock
and I watched "American Idol." I read the card on the
TV that described each channel on the motel's cable
service. I walked into the bathroom, removed the small
cakes of soap wrapped in waxy paper. I pulled back
the shower curtain and inspected the grimy tub behind
it. I shuffled through my bag and found the lonesome
embroidered sock. I returned to the bed and the lumpy
pillows in their weathered white pillowcases. I crumpled the sock in my hand, straightened out the creases
and then squeezed once more, like it was a stress ball.
Once more, I flipped channels and twirled the sock
around my index finger. I wondered if its owner had
thrown away the other one, or if she had held onto it,
hoping that one day she would find it under a bed or
stuck in a t-shirt pulled from the dryer. Maybe, when
she least expected, her missing sock would turn up in
the unlikeliest of places.

I planned to be at Misty's apartment before eight the
next morning. I could only assume that she still worked
in the business, maybe if not for Conroy. But if she
didn't, then she probably had a day job, and I wanted to
catch her before her commute.

    I stripped off the clothes I had fallen asleep in. I
drank water out of a plastic cup on the nightstand and
placed it next to the alarm clock. It was six forty-five,
just enough time for a shower and to try out a couple
of outfits. I grabbed the three I had hung on a rack
the night before. They still had wrinkles from being
packed. I thought about using an iron, but there wasn't
one in the closet and I didn't want to waste time call-
ing a housekeeper. And being sweaty and nervous, I

knew my clothes would just get rumpled on the drive to Misty's anyway. I hung my clothes on the bathroom door to let them steam work out the creases. I hopped in the shower and turned up the hot water.

When I was finished, I grabbed a towel and dried off. I stepped out of the shower. I shaved. I ran gel through my wet hair. I brushed my teeth. I applied lip balm. I slapped on deodorant, followed by lotion.

And I masturbated.

I did it methodically and with purpose. While I can't say it was without pleasure or that Misty did not enter my mind, I did it because I had no idea what might happen in the coming hours, and, if called upon, I wanted to be at my best. Afterward, the blood rushing to my face, I smiled and laughed because I felt no guilt. I had the feeling I would never have to do it again.

Unless she asked me to.

I opened the door from the bathroom and the thick steam from the shower collided with the cool air of the room. I stood in front of the full-length mirror in the tiny hallway next to the bathroom and looked at my reflection. I pushed back my hair and searched for flakes on my scalp. I scanned my body for blackheads, dried skin, wild hairs, crust in my eyes, wax in my ears, debris under my fingernails, lint between my toes. I noticed how much my long, bony shoulders and arms resembled the skeleton science teachers kept in the back of the classroom. I was embarrassed to compare myself to the men Misty knew on camera, how strong and sure they were, with big dicks and thick hair full of product. I flexed my arms, and only the faintest trace of bicep rose from the bone. I would never be beefy, I reasoned with myself, no matter how much I worked out, because I was naturally lanky. I saluted myself sarcastically and then put on a white t-shirt and my new favorite boxers, the ones with a martini glass pattern. A gift from Liz.

Traffic was so light, I practically coasted down Tenth Street to a parking garage near Misty's place. I pulled into a parking garage and found a tight spot between a delivery truck and a minivan. I squeezed out of the narrow opening, locked the door and moved away from the car. I inadvertently bumped the truck with my hip, which set off the vehicle alarm. The loud sound bounced around in the garage at a jarring, exaggerated decibel. I wiped off my pant leg, which I had scuffed squeezing by the truck, and ran down the stairs to the street below.

Misty lived in the kind of infill project the newspaper was always covering and the editorial page was always praising. It was a neighborhood where hipster art galleries, cafés, lofts and trendy boutiques were slowly crowding out the tattered bungalows, Chinese restaurants, laundries, shoe repair shops, liquor stores and bars. It was hard to tell which group Misty's apartment fit in. From a distance, it appeared newly renovated. It was painted creamy white, yellow and maroon, with an art deco, checkerboard pattern on the window sills. But up close, it was a different story. The paint was chipped, there were weeds and grass growing along the foundation and the swimming pool in the center of the complex was riddled with debris. I stopped at one of the galleries underneath the front apartments to view a bronze sculpture of a young ballerina on display, as good an excuse as any to linger, unnoticed, while I watched for Misty. A light flickered inside the gallery and a woman, possibly the owner, walked out from behind a curtain in the back. She rushed to the door, but I just smiled and waved her away. I pointed to the sculpture and raised my thumbs in approval as I went out to the sidewalk, walking the curb like a tight rope.

The entire hour I waited, I was taunted by the smell of coffee, baking bread and sausage from an English pub across the street. I hadn't eaten much. I was promised a continental breakfast by the motel's night clerk, but when I got to the lobby, it was nothing but a bowl of questionable fruit and stale coffee. I looked at my watch for the hundredth time. If Misty was coming out of her apartment complex, it wasn't for a nine-to-five gig. I decided I could watch for her from the patio at the pub. Besides, a little food might settle my nerves.

When I walked inside, the smell of breakfast was ruined by the stench of last night's liquor. There was a young family in the back of the restaurant, and they seemed strikingly out of place, like New York City tourists who had wandered into the Bronx. The parents sat across from each other in a booth toward the back. The mother gently fed her toddler son. The father looked like a businessman, the mother looked like she wanted to hide the fact that she was a stay-at-home.

A man at the bar hovered over a newspaper on the bar, a white towel slung over his shoulder. He looked preppy but tough, like he belonged in an Ralph Lauren ad, not a pub.

"Can I help you, friend?" His voice was gruff and raspy, like he'd been smoking since the cradle, but he must have been in his mid-twenties.

"Just a coffee, and maybe a muffin or something. Can I take it outside?"

"Sure thing. No muffins though. There's toast." He grabbed a cup and saucer and set it on the bar in front of me. He motioned to the back. "I've got a pot brewing. Just be a minute."

"I'm actually in a rush. Maybe I'll pass."

"Your choice. It'll just be a minute." He waited for me to decide. I looked through the stained glass window toward Misty's complex, craning my neck to see beyond the driveway on the adjacent street.

"Waiting for somebody?" the barman asked nonchalantly, as if it was a common occurrence at his place, people waiting and watching, never lingering for too long.

"No, not really. Sort of," I fumbled. Then I lied, for no reason at all. "I'm meeting my Realtor."

"That's cool. For one of them?" he asked, pointing to Misty's complex.

"Right, right, one of those," I said. "What do you think? Good neighborhood?"

"It's not bad, it's not bad. That used to be a real shit hole, but it's alright now."

I told him to skip the toast. I picked up the empty cup and said I'd take the coffee outside when it was ready. I put a couple bucks on the bar and left.

The sun had mostly risen and the bright light hovering over the horizon hurt my eyes and reminded me I was functioning on a fitful night's sleep. Wearily, I surveyed the apartments across the street, looking for signs of life. It was eerily quiet, very unlike Rancho Margarita.

The bar door swung open and hit me in the shoulder. I reached back and grabbed the handle, holding it open for the barman, who was carrying a nearly overflowing pot of coffee. His white towel was now draped over his arm like he was the grunge version of a waiter at a five-star restaurant.

"Here you go, man. Cheers," he said. An unlit cigarette hung out of his mouth. "Mind if I smoke out here with you?"

"I don't mind," I said, though actually, I did. I wasn't looking to be distracted. "But won't your customers miss you?"

His face contorted. "Oh, them?" he said, pointing back at the door. "Nah, they're here every morning. They own the place. Mom and dad sold it to 'em years ago."

"The family business, huh?" I kept an eye across the street as I spoke. He noticed, too.

"Not really. Didn't say I own it, did I?" He laughed. "That's my kid sis' in there. Just hers. And his."

I watched a car circle the block. I tried to make out the profile of the driver.

"Boy, you're really worried you're gonna miss her, huh?"

"What do you mean?"

"Your Realtor. You afraid she's gonna break that appointment or something?"

He took a long tug of his cigarette and blew out a plume of smoke. It seemed like he had more in his lungs but was holding on to it, the way a pot smoker held in a hit. He sounded constipated.

"There's a serious hottie that lives over there," he said, blowing out the remaining smoke.

"Oh, yeah?" I asked. I squinted my left eye the way Kristen did when she was glaring. "Interesting."

"Maybe you'll be neighbors. Hit that, bro."

"I don't know about that," I replied, unsure of who he was talking about. Of course he was talking about Misty.

"Yeah, man. She's kinky, too."

"I'm sorry." My voice cracked. "I don't follow."

"I heard she used to do porn. Nasty."

I wanted to lunge from my garden chair and punch him square in the face. Instead, I cleared my throat. My manly voice cracked. "Does she still?"

"Ah, you *are* interested."

"No, just curious. Never met someone like that."

"Who knows then, maybe today's your day. She's probably there. She don't go nowhere."

"That right?" I asked. Just then, a light gray Cadillac pulled up to the complex, and I saw my out. "Looks like that's her. Guess I better get going."

"Hold on," he said, "don't you want your coffee?"

I took a sip of the coffee, holding the cup with shaking hands. It was acidic and pungent. I smelled it again and then took another sip.

"Bourbon." He smiled. "On the house."

"Why?"

"Ah, why not?" he said. "You look like you could use it."

21

I straightened my tie before knocking on the door to Misty's apartment. I decided the maroon one went best with my black suit and brown dress shoes, both of which I had last worn to a funeral. I didn't want to come across as some fan. I wiped my palms on the sides of my wool pants, and I felt the sweat on my legs underneath. Summer in California was a terrible time to be wearing a wool suit. Every part of me was damp.

There was a low window next to the front door, just like at a motel. The pale linen curtains were drawn, so I peeked through a small crack at the bottom. All I could see was the back of a couch. I knocked on the door with my white knuckles.

A whisper came from behind the door. "Yes?" Her voice wasn't just gentle or shy. It was timid, the way an abused dog would sound if it could speak.

"We've never met," I said, "but my name is Ethan Ames."

She opened the door as far as the chain lock allowed, holding a cigarette, and it was like seeing a celebrity. She looked more like a caricature of herself than the actual person I'd spent all this time gazing at in a magazine. She was wearing a light yellow t-shirt, cutoff Levis and pink flip flops. She was heavier than in the photo, though her weight was evenly spread. Her hair, tied in a ponytail, looked like it hadn't been washed for days. A few strands hung untidily over her forehead, where makeup was meant to conceal light acne scarring along her hairline. Her eyes were dark around the edges, and her long lashes were clumped together by tiny flakes of mascara. When she took a drag of her cigarette, she sucked her cheeks into her mouth, making her appear gaunt and skeletal. But she was still kind of radiant. She still looked like the photo—with clothes on, of course.

"Sorry," she said, examining my attire, "I'm Catholic."

"No, it's not like that," I said. "I saw a picture of you and I wanted to meet you, that's all. I don't want to freak you out or anything." I paused. The corners of my mouth were gummy. My tongue clicked with every syllable. I was coming off exactly like the deranged fan I had tried so hard not to be.

She watched me like a hawk watched a mouse. I wondered if I had caught her at a bad time, because she seemed uncomfortable. But then she smiled and let me shake her hand. She held on for a moment. Whereas mine was sweaty, her hand was soft and cool. I savored that first touch.

"You came for a look?" She pointed to her body with both hands. I thought I heard a trace of cynicism in her voice. She fidgeted with the cigarette between her fingertips. "No, I suppose you came for a little more."

"Not at all."

She stepped out of the door and brushed off the dirt and dried leaves from a white plastic chair. She put the cigarette in her mouth and pointed to a chair across from her. I sat as directed, in awe of Indira.

"You from Sac'?" she asked.

"No. Just visiting."

"Oh. So what's your story? Where are you from?"

"Wyoming. I moved to California earlier this year."

"Why did you leave Wyoming?" she asked, but before I could answer, she nodded knowingly. "For a girl?"

"For a girl," I said. "Is that typical?"

"Yeah. You men follow your cocks." She said "cocks" unceremoniously.

"I'd like to think it was more than that. I'd like to think it was about love or something, too."

"Love or something, too," she repeated. "You still with her?" But before I could answer, she exhaled. "No, I bet not. Otherwise you wouldn't be knocking on my door."

She pulled on her cigarette, dropped it to the cement below and snuffed it with her flip flop. "I take that back. You could be here and still be with her. That would be about right."

"I'm not," I said, "still with her. You don't have a high opinion of men."

"Not really."

"I guess I can't blame you, I mean."

"Don't get me wrong," she said, "nobody made me fuck people for a living."

"So, Indira—"

"You know, my name's not really Indira," she said.

"I know."

"It's Misty."

"I know."

"I suppose you *do* know."

She put on a pair of wire-rim sunglasses pulled from her pocket and lit another cigarette. "So," she began, "where did you see me?"

I answered shyly. "*Tight Horizons.*"

Misty didn't remember the magazine, so she asked me to describe it. I didn't know how you could forget something like that. I would think every time you posed nude or had sex on cue, it would be memorable. But then again, I could barely stand naked in front of a mirror. Maybe if you were in front of cameras for long enough, specifics became vague.

"You were wearing red gingham," I said.

Misty looked as though she wanted to ask a question, but needed to think it through first. She flung her hair with her hand and sat forward in her chair. She wiped her eyes with her palms. "You have the picture?"

"I do." I hesitated. "In my bag."

I put my pack on the table and waited for Misty's signal. She nodded. I unzipped the top flap and nervously reached for the photo. It was stiff from where I had taped it together.

When I produced the picture, she snatched it out of my hands. I put the bag on the ground and folded my hands over my lap. She concentrated on the photo. Her fingers trembled.

"This was a long time ago."

"How long ago?" I asked.

"In this business, it was a *long* time ago. It seems like

forever to me."

"How long?" I asked again. I had to know.

"Three years, maybe? I thought I had a future ahead of me." Misty touched the tape with her thumb and folded the paper neatly along the original creases. She handed it back to me like it was a grade-school love note. The paper quivered in her hand. I took it and reached for my bag.

"You should throw that away," Misty stopped me, like a mother telling her child to ignore a dead bird on the sidewalk. "You don't want that."

"Alright." I put down my bag and walked over to a trashcan near the stairwell. I tore the folded page into several strips, and then tore those strips in thirds. I dropped the pieces of paper over the trashcan and watched them descend into the black garbage bag like snow falling on a tar pit. Indira may have been sitting behind me, but it felt like I was burying her.

"Thank you," she said as I returned to my seat. "So listen, I've got some stuff to do today. Want to come with?"

"Really? Are you serious?"

She looked confused, maybe annoyed. "Yes."

"Yeah. That would be great. Really."

Misty pulled a ring of keys from her pocket and locked her door. "Let's go then. My truck's just over there." I followed like a puppy on a string.

"You know, that was the only picture I had of you."

She smiled. "Don't worry, I'll get you another."

22

We walked across the street to her truck, a rusted red beater with oversized tires and raised hydraulics. Misty got in first and then leaned across the passenger seat to unlock my door. The truck's upholstery was a multicolored waffle pattern. A pair of black Ray Bans hung from sunglass straps around the rear view mirror. The top of the dashboard had a small crack in it, as did the windshield. The air inside smelled musty.

Misty turned on the vent and rolled down the window. Then she reached to the dial of an AM/FM radio and a tape deck, and I was pleased to see that my old Subaru wasn't the only car that lacked air conditioning and a decent stereo. She pressed the volume button and a tape churned inside.

"You like music?" she asked.

I nodded enthusiastically, recognizing a good opportunity for a little self-promotion.

"Yeah. I actually interned at *Record Shelves* in New York. I wrote for them, and everything."

Even if I was reciting my work history like it was a job interview, people usually found it notable. Everybody knew *Record Shelves*. Judging from the look on Misty's face, she seemed impressed.

"Do you still?" she asked.

"Write for them? Not really. Not in a while, I guess."

"Why not?"

"No reason, really," I said. "Well, a few reasons, I guess."

"The girl?"

"Isn't it always?" I meant it as a joke, but she took it seriously. I decided to change the subject.

"So how'd you get into porno?"

"Porno, that's a funny word. Not one way or the other. Kind of right down the middle." She said, parting the air with her hand. I stared out the window.

"I'm sorry," she said. "I didn't mean to hurt your feelings."

"You didn't," I assured her.

"Hold on," Misty yelled. She slammed the gas pedal and sped across the busy street into a left turn lane. We were going the wrong direction down a one-way. She braked, turned quickly and raced back toward the freeway.

"Sometimes I drive like I'm still in L.A." she said, wistfully. "I haven't gotten used to all these one-ways."

We barreled down the freeway, the shadows of overpasses sprinting across my lap. Misty was already speeding, but whenever a car passed us, she exhaled noisily and stepped on the gas pedal. When we exited at Sixty-Fifth Street, on the other side of Sacramento, I was relieved that we were slowing down.

"People call Sacramento a cow town," she said as we drove through patches of farmland surrounded by new business parks and industrial plants. "I can see that."

She turned in to the lot of a Catholic church and parked next to a clunky white minivan in a long row of beat-up Ford Crown Victorias, Chevy Cavaliers and Dodge Caravans. Two kids hopped out in front of the truck, but their mother prodded them away. She scolded them in Spanish as we got out. The mother then reached inside the van and produced two empty boxes, the top flaps folded inward. The little girl lined up next to her mother, and the boy leaned into her hip. He was short enough to stand under the boxes in his mother's arms. She raised her arm awkwardly to accommodate the both of them. The mother looked worn down by the chore of raising two small children, but she also seemed proud.

"I love kids," Misty said. "I have a couple nieces. They're like that."

"Do they live around here?" I asked.

"No, Orange County," she said.

"That's not too far." I followed Misty up the sidewalk to the church. "Do you go see them a lot?"

"Their mom doesn't let me much."

"Why?"

"I'm a bad example."

"Because of your work?"

"It's complicated. It's a sister thing."

She stopped talking when we came to the door, where a long line had formed.

"So what is this?" I asked.

"You couldn't tell?"

I looked around. There were elderly people, home-less people. Ahead of us were a few families similar to the one we saw coming in. I shrugged, unsure. "Food bank?"

She nodded modestly and then smacked her forehead. "Shit, I forgot the boxes in the truck. I gotta go back."

"I'll get them," I volunteered. "Hold onto your place in the line."

I hustled back to the truck and looked in the back of the bed. There were grass clippings, a tool kit and several cardboard boxes. I grabbed two and hurried back, but not before five people had lined up behind Misty.

"Wow, filling up fast," I said, out of breath. I handed her the smaller box and kept the larger for myself to carry.

"It goes quick around here."

When our turn came, we quickly surveyed the stacked canned goods neatly arranged along two folding tables. Most of the goods were rejects from suburban pantries: canned pumpkin from last year's Thanksgiving, generic peas and carrots, the random water chestnuts or jarred asparagus. I imagined the taste of limp, pallid asparagus and shivered. I pointed to the can and leaned over to Misty.

"Why not just put out beets?" I asked playfully.

Misty moseyed over to the second table, casually fingering the cans and bagged goods. She grabbed a can of beets, read the label and set it in her box. She returned wearing a satisfied grin.

"That's disgusting."

We were flirting, and we both immediately realized how strange that was. She turned back to the table and grabbed more cans.

One of the women behind the tables greeted Misty by name. Like the others, she wore a Hawaiian shirt, khaki pants and white SAS shoes. A wood cross dangled from a black string tied around her neck.

"Sister Josephine."

"Always so nice to see you, dear," the nun said. "Are you well?"

"Yeah." Misty glanced at me and continued talking with the nun. "How are you?"

"I saved you something." The nun reached under the table and produced a package of flour. Misty quickly put it in her box.

"For your baking," Sister Josephine said. She blocked her lips with the back of her hand and whispered so the others in line wouldn't hear. "It's organic."

Misty and Sister Josephine laughed, and then the nun turned to me very suddenly. "Misty is quite the baker."

"I didn't know that," I said.

"Why would you?" Misty replied sheepishly. "We just met this morning." She made eye contact with Sister Josephine while saying the last part. The nun nodded approvingly and then looked out over the table at the long line growing behind us. She stepped out from behind the table, put her hand on Misty's shoulder and gently swept her down a hallway. Misty listened politely while the nun spoke, occasionally nodding her head. They returned to the table several minutes later. Sister Josephine repositioned herself behind the sauerkraut, and Misty gave me a faint smile.

"It was nice to meet you, dear." The nun extended her hand.

"You, too. I'm Ethan, by the way."

"So I'm told." She smiled, squeezed my hand and then released it. "God bless you both, dears."

We carried our boxes outside, and I whispered into Misty's ear.

"They don't wear the nun hats?" I asked.

"No," she said, "they don't wear the *nun hats.*"

Once we were back in the rickety truck and on the freeway, I asked Misty what the nun had said in the hallway. She responded by turning up the radio.

"So... you bake?" I asked.

"Not really. I brought that nun some muffins once, from a bakery that gives away day-old stuff. Just as a thank you. I'm sure she knew they were store-bought. But she likes to encourage me."

"Encourage you how?"

"To find interesting things to do," Misty said. "To stay out of trouble."

I put my arm on top of the larger box jammed between us. I picked up the package of flour from the smaller box on my lap and read the nutrition chart on the back. I liked holding Misty's groceries.

"Funny, huh?" She nodded at the package. "Had to be organic."

"Yeah," I agreed, "in California, even the nuns are granolas."

"I have one more stop to make," Misty said, exiting the freeway. She pulled into a parking lot. I looked out from under the roof of the truck to see the sign high above. It was a drug store.

"I just need to grab some things," she said, unbuckling her seatbelt. She pulled the door latch, and when I did the same, Misty signaled for me to stop. "Just wait here, OK?"

I adjusted the box on my lap and got comfortable. Misty shut the door. I watched her walk up the parking lot. It was no wonder she'd been in porno. Misty looked great, even in what were evidently less prosperous times. She had a bubble butt, so the edges of her cutoff jeans hung away from her thighs, the loose strands tickling the tops of her legs. She walked through the store's sliding doors and disappeared.

I unrolled the window and felt a light breeze come into the cab. It was refreshing.

Forty-five minutes later, Misty emerged from the drug store carrying several small, white paper bags, all of which where folded and stapled shut. Misty opened the door and tossed the packages under her seat. As she backed out, a Honda hatchback zipped in behind us, forcing Misty to slam on the brakes.

"Oh, shit," Misty screeched. "Sorry," she said in the. rearview mirror.

The driver shouted something we couldn't hear with his windows rolled tight. It sure looked like swearing, though. The driver had a thin goatee, long hair pulled back into a ponytail and wire-rim glasses. He pounded the horn on his steering wheel with the butt of his hand. I unrolled my window and stuck out my head.

"Give it a rest, you dirty fucking hippy!" I shouted as loud as I could. People standing in front of the drug store turned around. The driver shrunk in his seat. Misty found first gear, ran a stop sign at the parking lot exit and took the nearest on-ramp.

"'Dirty fucking hippy?'" she asked.

"You don't think that was too mean?"

She laughed and checked a digital clock pasted on

the top of her dashboard. It was the kind a credit card company sends as a gift if you pay shipping and handling.

"Think you have time to go to my place?" she asked.

"Yeah," I said, sitting up. "Of course."

"Good. I have something I want to show you."

23

The window above Misty's kitchen sink was open, and the smell of oleander and roses from outside stifled the staid odor of cigarette smoke. Misty kicked off her flip flops in the direction of the coat closet and strolled happily in her bare feet. I asked if I should also remove my shoes, and when she shook her head, I was relieved. I was wearing my only dress socks, and one had a hole in the toe.

The vinyl floor was covered with shag rugs and out-of-fashion designer furniture. There was a dusty glass vase filled with carved wood flowers on the coffee table. Waxy green plants clung to the edges of windows where sunlight crept in, the unexposed sides yellowing from a lack of attention. A bookshelf in the living room was filled with garish romance novels and children's coloring books. Above was a shelf piled with teddy bears. When we walked in, Misty corrected one that had fallen on its side.

There was a framed picture of two kids hung on the

wall, as well as a picture of an older woman with short, curly white hair. I assumed she was Misty's mother. She had Misty's nose and tired eyes. She looked kind. She looked like she cooked good casseroles and told funny stories.

Misty went into a bedroom and shut the door behind her, and I fantasized that she was putting on lingerie. I took a seat on the couch in front of the TV. The cushions sunk under my weight, and I unearthed pennies, crumbs and a remote from between them. I grabbed the remote and placed it on an end table.

"I found your remote," I said. "Did you miss it?"

"Good," she hollered from behind the door.

Misty came out of the bedroom carrying a videotape. She put the tape in the VCR, grabbed the remote and then sat on the other end of the couch. She hit play, and as the tape churned, I reveled in the proximity we were sharing.

She turned on the TV, and the first image we saw was one woman pulling down another's panties and grabbing at her shaved crotch. She fast-forwarded through the scene, which turned out to be all lesbian, and released the button on a black frame. The next scene began with Indira, her legs spread on a conference table, a guy with a short mullet sticking his tongue in her vagina, flicking it quickly back and forth. I heard the moan of familiar vocal chords. I squirmed on the couch as I stiffened. I tried to fight it, not that it mattered. Misty was focused on the screen.

"You didn't want to leave here without a picture," she said, watching each frame intently, "and now you've got it."

I tried not to watch. I forced my eyes in any direction other than that of the TV. Sitting next to Misty, watching her on the video, I felt like an intruder.

"This isn't exactly what I came here for," I mumbled, my lips barely moving, like a novice ventriloquist.

"Isn't it?"

Misty pointed back at the screen. Indira was on her back now, rubbing her large breasts with clenched hands, her legs spread even wider. Her partner moaned and moaned and then withdrew, spilling on her stomach as he went. Indira then drew him to her mouth, and I heard Misty gulp as though she might vomit. Afterward, he smeared what was left across her smiling face, and when it was over, I felt such shame, I couldn't breathe.

"I used to like it," Misty said matter-of-factly as she wiped her eyes. She stared straight ahead at the TV, the screen flickering. It had been so long since I'd been around a VCR, I didn't realize it was still turning until it made a startling mechanical noise and snapped into rewind. "I really did. I mean, come on, you don't get into it if you don't like it. There's something inside you that makes you want to do it, you know?"

I couldn't find words.

"Kind of different now," she said.

Misty rose from the couch and paced in the middle of the room. She cupped her hands together and fidgeted with the knuckle of her ring finger. Outside, a garbage truck moved along the side of the road, lifting the bins with its loud hydraulics and warning beeps sounding danger. Emptied, the mechanical arm brought the bin back down to earth, each landing with a violent thud. Off in the distance, an alarmed dog barked. Misty glanced out the window.

"How do I look to you? Do I still look pretty?" She moved closer to me. "Not pretty like I did there, I know. I look different now."

"I think you look beautiful," I said. "Very beautiful."

Misty continued to move closer, and I found myself shrinking in the corner of the couch. She got down on her knees and crawled. She put her hands on my thighs and spread my legs. Her heavy breasts rubbed against my crotch, and I could feel the extra weight she had put on underneath them. Her face was increasingly close to mine, and her lips quivered as they neared. My ears felt hot and my neck felt cold. Chills ran down my spine. Her hot breath brushed my cheek. It smelled fruity, like cranberry juice.

"You still want to fuck me, right?"

I supposed she didn't really want an answer, a good thing, since I didn't have one to give. We both knew what I wanted. Why else had I sought her out? Why had I, really?

Misty picked herself up off the floor. She stood before me, parting the shag rug with her toes, her leg pointed forward like a ballerina. Then she went into the kitchen. I heard her rummaging around, and when she came back, she brought a smoldering cigarette and a diet soda. She did not ask me if I wanted one, but just stared out the window, smoking, drinking. She watched the garbage truck go down the street.

"I guess I should get going?" I asked, knowing she wanted me to leave. I was confused; it wasn't my idea to watch that video. I hadn't asked for it. Or maybe I had.

"I think so."

"Alright."

Misty escorted me to the door with her hand on my elbow. "It was nice to meet you," she said, strangely, with a note of encouragement. "I used to love seeing my fans, signing autographs. I don't see many fans anymore."

She put on her sunglasses and followed me down the stairs to the gates of the complex, where she waited patiently while I figured out a good way to say good-bye. I finally asked if I could give her a hug. She said yes. When I pulled away, Misty reached into her grubby shorts pocket.

"This is for you," she said, holding out a photo. I touched her fingers as I took it.

"Who is this?" I asked, confused.

"It's me," she said. "That's what I used to look like."

24

Liz answered the door wearing a loose blouse and tight bootcut jeans, the frayed cuffs draped over her bare feet. She looked sleepy and uncertain.

"So," she asked neutrally, "how did it go?" We were still standing at the entryway of her house.

"I think you know." I had a lot of time to think on the way back from Sacramento. I knew Liz had gotten Misty's address—and her story—from Conroy. I even entertained the idea that Liz was only with Conroy to help me find Misty, but I knew I was lying to myself. I did that a lot.

I stepped inside and closed the door. I put a hand behind Liz's neck and brought her closer. I thought she might resist, but when I kissed her, she kissed right back. I put my hand under her shirt at the small of her back. I caressed her neck and brought my fingers to the small opening between her jeans and her skin. I pushed them into her panties and moved them around to the front of her waist, unbuttoning the top of her jeans as she closed her lips around mine.

And then she pulled away. I brought her close again, but she resisted and began to button her jeans. I moved to undo them, but she was firm.

"What's wrong?" I asked, breathing heavily. I pushed my hair out of my eyes and then took her by the waist once more. She kissed me one last time, squeezing her face against mine, and then moved past my lips and to my ear. She wrapped her arms around my neck.

"I'm not her," she whispered.

Liz waited on the couch while I collected my things. I haphazardly folded my clothes and placed them on top of the CDs in my hockey bag. Liz rattled off a checklist of trivial items I might have forgotten: my travel-sized toothpaste, an old plastic Fast Mart cup, a tattered copy of *Record Shelves*. My picture of Indira.

"No, I'm good," I told her as I carried the heavy bag to the door. "I've got it."

When we stepped outside, I pointed to the Speedster. "I just filled it and checked the oil." A chunk of sunlight bounced off the chrome fender. "It's a good car. Take care of it."

"I will. Are you sure you don't need a ride?"

I wasn't sure, actually. But we both understood it was time.

"No, I'm good. It'll be alright. It's nice and cool tonight."

"Where are you going to go?"

"I hear there's a nice Motel 6 down the street." We both laughed a little, and then I walked down the stairs. We didn't hug goodbye.

"Hey, Ethan," Liz yelled from the top of the stairs.

I turned around and looked up, my hand held over my eyes like a visor. I remembered the first time I had seen Liz up there, drunk, waiting for me to find her keys. I thought about what I had seen then, and what I saw now. The sun was setting, and the fiery red light glowed beautifully behind the wisps of her auburn hair.

"I'll keep an eye out for your byline," she said.

25

A couple weeks later, I found work as a reporter at a small daily in Hemet, much to the delight of my dad. But I was delighted, too. It felt good to be writing again, even if my beat was a little scattered. In my first week, I covered a robbery, two house fires, and a spelling bee for senior citizens. I even covered a parade, a first for this small-town reporter. Several float riders threw candy onto the streets, and I picked up a few pieces. My first bribe. I wrote a glowing story.

I stepped onto the patio of my one-bedroom apartment for my nightly ritual, a bottle of wine in hand. I put it down on an old TV tray I had bought at a nearby thrift store because it reminded me of one from my childhood. The tray was covered with a cloth napkin stolen from Kristen. I lit several candles and placed them on the tray. Then I leaned the picture of Misty against the bottle. Her face came and went under the gentle flicker of flames. Every time I filled my glass, she tipped over, but I always made sure to put her back where she belonged.

I spent a lot of the time out there thinking of story ideas or flipping through old editions of the newspaper, though by the end of the night, usually drunk, I reminisced on past events.

I never did hear what happened to Eddie. I called his cell a few times, but it always went to voice mail, and then, one day, was disconnected. I felt bad about Eddie losing his job, but maybe he considered it a favor.

Clark e-mailed to tell me that he had entered my front-page design in the CAL Awards, and that one of them had taken third. He offered to mail me the certificate. I told him I was in no hurry, that I had even better news.

"Glad to hear about the new job," he wrote back. "The smut business never suited you, Ethan. Better to leave it to the professionals."

Liz and I spoke occasionally, but it was mostly e-mail and text messages. But I continued to read her reporting online. It was as sharp as ever. I fantasized that she also read mine.

Sufficiently buzzed, I took a deep, cleansing breath. The cool desert air was nothing like it was at Liz's place. Forever now, ocean air would remind me of her. I collected the contents from the tray, the bottle and glass in one hand, the picture of Misty in the other, the napkin bunched under my arm. I pulled open the sliding door with my foot and carried everything through the living room and into the kitchen. As I headed back toward the patio to lock the door, I noticed something on the carpet in the middle of the room. I flipped a light switch. It was the nylon sock I had found at the Motel 6. It must have gotten stuck to the napkin when

I pulled it out of the dryer. I picked it up and ran my fingers over the stitches of the embroidery like an Arab methodically stroking his worry beads.

On Friday, I quickly filed my daily assignment and weekend enterprise so I could surf the Internet or play solitaire the rest of the day. I stared into my computer screen and contemplated what I might do over the weekend with no ex-girlfriends to contend with, no foxy star reporters to tease me, no porno stars to track down.

"Stories already in, huh?" asked my editor, Bob, standing over my desk in the middle of the newsroom. "You keep this up, you're not going to have any friends in the newsroom. Well, except me, and I'm in good with the guy who signs your check, so I'm probably the only friend you need."

"Thanks, Bob. My dad taught me there's nothing wrong with filing early. I guess it's a good habit."

"He did you a service. You've done a good job this week, Ethan. I'd like to buy you lunch."

"Sure," I said.

He grabbed his worn corduroy sport coat off the back of his chair and pulled it over his sea-green button down. Both looked like they were from the Sears clearance rack. None of us were getting rich in Hemet; most of the reporters were there on a brief stop before finding a better paycheck elsewhere. But Bob was a true believer. He reminded me of my dad with his industriousness, his bad jokes, his teaching methods. Coaching hotshot reporters who didn't think they needed it.

We exited the newsroom and went into the busy lobby, where the ladies at the front desk were diligently answering phones like they were operators from the 1950s. We hadn't even made it to the glass doors when one of them flagged down Bob with an urgent call. Stop the presses.

"I've got to take this, Ethan. Listen, you know Rose's Café down the street on Second?" he asked. "Why don't you grab us a table. Go ahead and order me a Rosie burger, extra mayo for the fries, and a coffee. Make sure the coffee's hot. You writing this down?"

I raised my eyebrows and he burst into laughter. "I'm kidding. I do love razzing you cubbies, I really do."

He patted me on the back and nudged me toward the door. "Get a Rosie burger, Ethan. Mix that ketchup and mayo, delicious. A heart attack, but heck, this whole existence is a heart attack, right?" Bob grabbed the phone from the receptionist, who was patiently waiting to pass along the caller.

I walked into Rose's, and a bell jingled overhead. The owner, Rosie—it was written on her nametag—seated me in the corner. While I waited for service, I crumpled a corner of the paper doily underneath my empty coffee cup. The place was old, with wood-paneled walls and uneven, linoleum-covered floors. But it wasn't so much rundown as it was well used, the kind of place that might alienate the regulars if it ever underwent a renovation. Every small town with a newspaper had a diner just like it, filled with old men wearing flannels and suspenders, drinking their coffee from dated ceramic mugs. Gabbing and laughing, coughing and wheezing.

"You want some coffee? Green tea?" asked a waitress who was holding two steaming pots. She was thin, and her scrappy reddish hair was cut at different lengths like a pixie. She had deep, dark eyes, fair skin and a few freckles on her nose and cheeks. She looked like she might be a couple years younger than me. She looked familiar.

"No, thanks. Just some water."

"No coffee? That's a first around here. Of course, somebody my age coming in here is a first, too. Are you going for that ironic thing?" She snapped the gum in her mouth, like she was a waitress at a roadside diner. It was cute. "You need a trucker hat. There's an American Eagle in Temecula."

I laughed. "I guess there aren't a lot of people our age around here."

The door jingled, and the waitress looked over at the new customer. I took the opportunity to scan her nametag, but the print had mostly faded from the black plastic.

"Were you ready to order?"

"I'm waiting for somebody, but I guess he knows what he wants."

"OK, shoot."

"He'd like something called a Rosie burger. Mayo for the fries. Oh, and a coffee."

"Newspaper editor?"

"Yeah. How did you guess?"

"You get to know people around here. All these guys," she said, scanning the room, "they order the same thing every day. I can tell you what each of them gets. It's kind of sad, really. Monotony!" She groaned. "Sometimes I wonder why I even came up here. Anyway, that one," she said, pointing to a guy wearing a John Deere cap, a plaid shirt and cowboy boots, "he always gets the biscuits and gravy. Nothing special, right?"

"No, I don't suppose so. A lot of guys probably get that."

"*Right.* But then he asks for sliced pickles on top of it." She shuddered, puckering her lips like she had just bitten into a slice of lemon. "Disgusting, huh? He *counts* them, too. Gotta have twelve pickles on there, otherwise he sends it back."

"Seriously?"

"They're all like that. The coffee has to be scalding. The apple pie has to have cheese melted on top of it—and not just cheese, but *American* cheese. I mean some even tell me it *has* to be Kraft. It's weird. What's with you men?"

"We're born with obsessive-compulsive disorder." The pop psychology was meant to be a joke, but she seemed to take it seriously.

"Maybe," she said. "So what's your thing?"

"What do you mean?"

"What's your special order, OCD boy?" She was pleased with my new moniker.

"Let's see, I couldn't tell you off the top of my head. I guess mine isn't food. I was just going to order the same thing the boss is having, you know? Maybe hold the mayo."

"Interesting. Maybe that's your OCD—'I'll have what the boss is having,'" she said in a mocking baritone. "'And a side of brown nosing, too!'" She reached over the table and pinched me teasingly.

"OK," I said, accepting her challenge. "I'll have a Coke."

"One Coke," she wrote on her pad. "I'm very proud of you. A small step, but a brave one."

"Thanks for the encouragement."

The waitress took a look around the restaurant. Rosie was still busy with a few customers at the counter, but otherwise, it seemed like the lunch rush was over.

"Mind if I sit for a minute?" she asked.

I gestured to the chair across from me. "If you don't think Rosie will mind."

"She won't." The waitress set the hot pots down on a napkin on the table. "Hey, did you know that's not even her real name?"

"I didn't."

"Yeah," she nodded. "Her real name is Margaret. The Rose up there in the sign, that's actually her grandma. Sometimes you'll see her roaming the kitchen all quiet, but then she always scurries back upstairs. They all live up there."

"Why does she go by Rosie then?"

"'Cause that's what people call her." She shrugged. "So tell me what's it like working at the paper? They pay well?"

"Not really."

"Too bad. You seem like a guy who should be making some money by now." I thanked her, assuming she meant it as a compliment.

"I'm in a transition right now."

"Hemet's the place for a transition," she said. "I'm in a bit of a transition myself."

"Oh yeah? From what?"

"Aren't you curious?" she said, playfully.

I prodded her with raised eyebrows.

"I moved up here with my dad. He just transferred to a new job, basically forced me to come with him. It was probably a good thing, though. I was getting into trouble. But I'm making some changes." She slapped the top of my hand. "But, oh, my God, can you believe how boring Hemet is!"

She rose from her chair. "Anyway, I better get back to work. What was your name?"

"Ethan," I said. "Ethan Ames."

"Ethan Ames," she said aloud as she scribbled my name on her pad. "I'll have to keep an eye out for your byline."

I looked at her name tag again, and in a different light I could see it was Linda. She saw that I was looking at the name tag and covered it with her hand.

"Ignore that. It's not mine," she said in a hushed voice. "I keep losing mine. I don't know who Linda is!" She seemed pleased to be someone else for a day. "How does someone get the name Linda anyway? Can you imagine a baby named *Linda*?"

"No, I can't."

"I mean, *jeez*, the poor kid! And never mind the high school years."

"So what is it?"

"It's Bethany." She held out her hand. There were orders written in blue ink on her palm. "Let me go put in your order." She trotted over to the kitchen window and placed the order on the ticket wheel. She looked cute in her sparkling white uniform and low-top Chucks, which were crowned with mismatched socks. One was a white cotton ankle sock, but the other was thin nylon in two shades of blue, a flowery design stitched above the ankle. I recognized it right away. The match was in my hockey bag.

Bethany returned with my Coke, which she placed on the table along with Bob's coffee and two ice waters. The carbonation bubbles jumped onto my face.

"I don't know if you're aware of this, Bethany, but your socks don't match."

Her face was red. "I know. Rough morning." She put her leg forward and pointed her foot. She reached down and rubbed her fingers across the embroidery.

"My grandma gave them to me when I was a kid. She did the stitch work herself. Hardly fits now, but so what? I think everyone should have flowers on their socks, don't you?"

"Maybe. Might be a little weird in my case," I joked.

"Well, I do." Bethany studied the embroidery, like she might find a stitch she hadn't noticed before.

"Anyway, I lost the other one. That makes me really sad. But I can't throw this one out, you know? Or put it in the rag basket or whatever you do with an orphaned sock."

"Why not?"

"I just love it too much," she said. "Besides, I think the other one is still out there, waiting for me to find it."

"You do?"

"Sure I do," she said. "Ethan, don't you believe in fate?" Her eyes twinkled.

The front door opened with a jingle. I didn't realize it was Bob until he was at our table.

"Sorry it took me so long, Ethan. Another dropped subscription, damn it. Excuse me dear," he said, moving past Bethany to take the chair in front of her. "Say, can you warm this up, sweetheart?" Bob asked, handing her his cup. "Go ahead and stick it in the microwave for a minute. I like it scalding, you know what I mean?"

Bethany nodded. She knew exactly what he meant.

"I mean hot!"

"Sure." Bethany wasn't looking at Bob when she answered. "I'll go check on your burgers, too." She took his cup and walked over to the counter.

Bob gulped his glass of water. "So!" he said, wiping his mouth with the sleeve of his jacket. He leaned forward over the table, rubbing his hands together like he had just come in from a blizzard. "Think you'll find your way in our humble little town, Mr. Ames?"

"I might," I said, watching the order wheel turn round and round. "I just might."

Eric Rohr began his career as an intern at *Rolling Stone*, later writing for the magazine and its website. He has since worked as a reporter, editor and graphic designer. He lives in Davis, California, with his wife and son. *Gingham Blindfold* is his first novel.

3559874

Made in the USA